a HANDYMAN for The Heart

a HANDYMAN for The Heart

Can Stephanie learn to follow God's plan when it isn't her own?

Beth Bulmer-Sirois

Thomas-john Veilleux

Tate Publishing & *Enterprises*

This title is also available as a Tate Out Loud product. Visit www.tatepublishing.com for more information.

Published by Tate Publishing & Enterprises, LLC
127 E. Trade Center Terrace | Mustang, Oklahoma 73064 USA
1.888.361.9473 | www.tatepublishing.com

Tate Publishing is committed to excellence in the publishing industry. The company reflects the philosophy established by the founders, based on Psalms 68:11,
"The Lord gave the word and great was the company of those who published it."

Cover design by Eddie Russell
Interior design by Jennifer L. Fisher

Published in the United States of America

ISBN: 978-1-60247-921-0
1. Christian: Fiction
2. Romance: Contemporary
07.08.27

For Jesse...

Stephanie Meets Russell

Snow fell on the small town of Belgrade Lakes, Maine, where Stephanie Gallagher stood outside her parents' home and gazed across the foothills that surrounded Belgrade Village. In the distance were pine trees standing fluently among houses that took advantage of spacious views across a wide lake. Several businesses along the water's edge remained boarded up with plywood and lumber that protected their windows and doors from harsh Maine winters. It was a quiet time of year in the small community, and Stephanie reminisced of the thousands of tourists that drew in from all over the world each new summer.

For the most part, Stephanie loved living in Belgrade Lakes. She especially liked the fact that she could enjoy all four seasons in a town where neighbors knew each other well and called each other by first name. To her, this was home, and the lake that typically shimmered brightly with speckles of warm summer sun lay undisturbed by a blanket of snow and ice. Stephanie watched from her parents' porch as a few cross-country skiers passed across the frozen lake. In the chilly, damp air, there was a silence about the community; and the area was peaceful, except for an occasional snowmobile racing across wide-open spaces and the sound of a north wind blowing through the trees.

To the south of the lake were smelt shacks busy with anglers, as wood smoke poured from their tiny tin chimneys. It was ice-fishing season in Belgrade, and the high point for winter businesses. The local sportsman's shop that normally sold scuba diving equipment and Jet Ski rentals during summer months was home to some of the best fishing tackle around. Stephanie was not fond of ice fishing, yet she enjoyed a home cooked meal of fresh smelts dipped in corn meal and fried to perfection.

From the hillside where the Gallagher's Victorian home was perched, Stephanie could view almost anything in the village. Winter months stripped all but a few remaining leaves from oak trees that separated her yard from the street below. She watched patiently as a gust of wind threatened to take the last few remaining leaves from the trees that provided shade during the summer over an old rope swing. Behind her was the house she adored more than any other home. Her bedroom was on the second floor above the front porch, with a window overlooking the lake. Her parents raised her from an infant in this house, and it was here she learned about family values.

Melva, Stephanie's mother, often reminded her of the stormy winter night Stephanie came into the world. It was nearly seventeen years earlier when a storm broke out and brought forth a record-setting snow. Blizzard winds knocked down power lines, and snow covered the roads in as much as four feet with snowdrifts. Her mother gave birth to her that night in the living room as her grandparents helped in the delivery.

Stephanie found her parents' stories amusing and wondered what it must have been like on that stormy night. Melva told her it was a miraculous birth, but Stephanie liked to believe that all births were miracles. The light from candles and heat from an old woodstove were all they had to stay warm that night. Grampy Marsh heated water in kettles on the stove while Grammy Marsh coached Melva in her breathing. Melva was a champion that night as she gave birth to Stephanie, who doctors later said weighed less than six pounds at the time of her birth. Indeed, it was nothing short of a miracle, especially since nearly two days had passed before baby Stephanie was able to see a doctor. Roads were dangerous due to the snow and wind, and Stephanie's father was away on business. It was, by all standards, a very old-fashioned birth. Stephanie knew it was because of God's grace she had grown to become the woman she was today.

As Stephanie stood outside, a sharp gust of wind sent chills down her spine. She had to laugh at herself for standing in the yard wearing nothing more than an unbuttoned coat, pajamas and slippers. Goose bumps did not discourage her from taking in all that the day had to offer. In the distance were faint sounds of snowmobiles winding across Salmon Bend, and just for a moment, the sun pierced through an overcast sky long enough for her to feel warm again.

The day held fair weather as a dusting of snow had fallen across the area that previous night, and the sky was a pale blue as scattered clouds blotted out the sun. Stephanie had planned to meet her parents at their workplace after school, and it seemed to be the perfect day for the walk. Her father, Paul, was the founder of a construction company called Paul's of New England while her mother Melva took care of the financial aspects of the company. They had started the business just months after Stephanie was born, and with the help of Paul's friend Alan, the two had managed to make the business a success. To Stephanie, Alan was more like an uncle. Though she knew little about him, she knew she could always count on him for a good laugh or cordial

"Hello." Alan was her father's business partner and friend, which made him special to her. Coincidentally, the building where their business operated from was just a few miles away from home. Stephanie enjoyed afternoon walks to the place her parents and Alan had built. The one-level building served as both a contractor garage and office. It was there she would meet with her parents on rare occasions and then ride home with them in the evenings. On this day, things did not go as planned…

Winter sunsets came at about four o'clock in the afternoon, and Stephanie walked quickly to avoid being out after dark. It was common for her to pray while she walked. She thought deeply about her future and gave thanks to the Lord for all He had done for her. She looked forward to graduating from high school, attending college, and some day following her parents' example for success. She was certain she would earn a degree, find a job, and then marry Tom Cruise… or *someone like him,* she thought with a smile. She knew marrying Tom Cruise would never happen, but she enjoyed entertaining the idea just the same. For Stephanie, she knew the future would be whatever God made it and that it was important for her to give the Lord her very best.

Straight ahead, Stephanie could see the lights of the tan sheet metal garage where her parents' business was located. There was a small paved parking lot in the front, and around the back of the structure, a four-bay garage with tall industrial doors. The garage section of the building, which towered over the office area, serviced heavy equipment trucks that carried tools and crewmembers to different job sites throughout the state.

Stephanie arrived just as the sun set below the horizon. It was getting dark; however, the lights that shined from the garage windows offered comfort, and she looked forward to getting into the warm, lighted environment. As she walked through the front door of the main office, she expected the normal greeting she always received. More often than not, Julie the receptionist was there at the front desk to say, "Hi." On this day, however, Julie was nowhere in sight.

Stephanie walked in the front office and looked around thinking that her parents or someone would soon enter the room. Perhaps her parents were down the hall.

"Hello?" she called.

There was no reply.

"Hello?"

No one responded.

From down a long hallway, Stephanie could hear the sound of a radio playing. It sounded as though it was coming from the garage located in the back. Curiously, she looked down the hallway that led to her mother's office. She was sure that at any moment a familiar face would be seen coming down that hallway. Yet, there was not. Something was odd. *Where was that greeting?* she wondered. *Where are my parents?*

There had always been somebody there to greet her. Somebody was always at the front desk. The building appeared to be empty, and it puzzled her.

"Hello?" Stephanie called out.

There was no answer.

"Hello?" she asked. "Is anybody here?"

Still, there was no answer.

"Mom?" she called.

As Stephanie turned the corner to see where the music was coming from, she could hear that it was coming from the garage. There was a glass door separating the garage from the offices, and it seemed creepy to her that the music would be playing if the building were empty. There was a light coming from her mother's office halfway down the hall on the right which was an immediate relief to her. She assumed that her mother was probably in the office meeting with Julie, then proceeded down the hall to greet them. As she came closer to the office door, she had expected to hear familiar voices, but there were none. She was afraid of interrupting something important, yet it became clear that her mother's office might be empty. As she stood in the doorway looking into the room, she was surprised to see her mother's high-back leather chair facing the back wall. *She must be on the phone,* Stephanie thought, then entered the room quietly. She wanted to surprise her mother by being there when she hung up the phone.

Inside Melva's office was a large shelf that held family photos and various knickknacks. To the right, there were chairs and a conference table. This was a common place where Stephanie and her mother would often visit and have lunch together. She walked over to the table and sat down without making a sound.

There was a rocking motion of her mother's chair, and Stephanie thought it was unusual that she could not hear her mother's voice. She thought that her mother might be on the phone with an important client, but then suddenly noticed that the phone was on the hook and not in use. For a moment, she contemplated surprising her mother by walking over to the desk and wiggling the back of her chair. Just as she was about to stand up, she was startled when the high-back leather chair quickly swung around. She was stunned to see a man she had never seen before. She jumped up. "Ah!" she screamed.

The man looked surprised to see Stephanie. He quickly stood up out of the chair. She had never seen anyone in her mother's chair before. This was a *very* unusual occurrence. Stephanie quickly realized something was terribly wrong.

"Who are you, and where are my parents!" she yelled. Her knees felt weak.

The man stood looking dumbfounded. He was a good deal taller than she was which seemed intimidating. Speechless, he fumbled for words to say. Stephanie feared the worse. She stepped back, and stood behind the conference table. The man looked confused and walked out from around the desk. This made her nervous because, in a flash, she realized that he had managed to come between her and the door. She had no place to escape. Quickly, she looked to the right and her mother's coffee maker sitting on a stand. It was on, and the coffee pot at least half-full. She knew this could be her only defense if the man attacked her. She reached for the hot coffee pot. "Who are you, and what were you doing in my mother's chair?" she yelled.

The man attempted to speak, still having trouble to find the words. "It's okay," he said.

"Where's my mother?" she yelled. "What'd you do to my parents?"

The man stood speechless, and held his hands in the air. He shook his head. Stephanie looked at the door and tried to estimate if she could get away from him. Her thoughts ran ramped, and she felt ill by the realization that he may have done something terrible to her parents. She knew she needed to defend herself.

"Come any closer and I'll hit you with this," she said, as she picked up the scalding coffee pot and held it by the handle with a tight fist-like grip.

"It's all right," the man said.

His calmness toward the situation scared her more. Her throat went dry, and the progression of hyperventilation set in. It felt to her as though every breath would be her last. Panic started to take over. She knew there would not be enough oxygen in the room to fight him. He was tall and obviously husky.

"Stay where you are!" she yelled.

"You don't know who I am?"

Before he could utter another word, Stephanie attempted to scream. She could barely make a sound. Her eyes filled with terror. She threw the hot pot of coffee at him with all her might. The man quickly ducked, and the coffee pot smashed into the wall knocking down her mother's diploma.

"Hey!" he yelled. "I'm just trying to tell you, I'm Alan's son."

Just at that time, Stephanie's mother came running into the room. She was shocked to see her daughter standing with a frightful look on her face.

"What was that racket?" Melva asked.

"Thank God, you're all right!" Stephanie yelled, and then ran to her mother's protective arms. She cried in relief as she gave her mother a big hug.

Melva held her daughter as she looked around the room. Realizing what had just happened, she calmly said, "So, I see you two have met."

Confused, Stephanie lifted her head from her mother's chest to look up. The man who she thought was about to attack her suddenly looked weary and frightened.

"Are you all right?" Melva asked.

Russell shrugged his shoulders feeling blameful for what had happened.

Melva looked at him. "Russell, this is my daughter, Stephanie." Then, she held her head back to look at her daughter. "Stephanie, this is Russell."

Stephanie glanced over at the man she had thought was going to attack her. She felt ashamed for overreacting.

Russell spoke. "I think I surprised her when she came in the room and saw me in your chair. I never heard her come in. I apologize." He then turned his eyes toward Stephanie hoping to make eye contact. She looked up at him for a brief second. "I'm sorry," he said to her.

All at once, Stephanie remembered hearing long ago that her father's business partner, Alan, had a son named Russell.

Ironically, she had never met Russell... until now. She glanced up at him for a second look. He was an attractive man in his mid-twenties with emerald green eyes and blond hair.

Stephanie spoke to her mother. "I didn't know who he was, and nobody was here... and what was I supposed to think?"

Melva asked, "Did you try looking in the garage?"

"No," Stephanie replied with embarrassment.

"Well, that's where I was. Your father put a new radio in his truck and he wanted me to hear it. He's still down there tinkering with it, but I'm surprised he didn't come running in here with the sound of all the commotion you two were making."

Russell looked at Stephanie with shame and embarrassment. "I'm sorry if I scared you," he said.

Stephanie did not say much, despite his concerted effort to make amends.

"I was going to introduce myself," he said. "But, when you grabbed that coffee pot, I was in shock." Russell tried to smile in light of the situation. "I'm sorry if I frightened you," he said.

Stephanie looked up at him as she let go of her mother. "No, no... I'm sorry," she said. "It's my fault." She felt silly for what had happened. "It was just a misunderstanding," she said.

Melva looked down and saw her coffee pot smashed all over the floor and coffee dripping down the wall. "Who's going to clean up this mess?" she asked.

Stephanie and Russell spoke up at the same time. "I will," they both said.

Stephanie quickly went over to her mother's cleaning supply closet, which was next to the conference table. The relief that the incident had ended without anyone getting hurt made her happy. She now knew her mother was all right, and that this man named Russell was no more than Alan's son. It felt strange to be in a room with him after what had happened, yet she was thankful that Russell was a good man, and she knew this would be something she would talk about for decades.

At the closet, Stephanie reached for the door handle and pulled the door open. Russell stood there eager to help. She looked over at him and curiously wondered what he must be thinking of her, after what she had done. She could see he was a good man and felt badly for almost killing him. As she opened the closet door, a broom handle fell forward. Stephanie reached up to keep it from falling, but Russell was quick to block the falling broom from striking her. Both reached up at the same time, and their hands oddly landed on the broom handle in the same place. Russell's right hand firmly covered hers, and she was surprised to feel the warmth of his hand embracing her.

Stephanie's Birthday

Stephanie was like most girls her age on the day she turned eighteen. It was springtime in Belgrade Lakes, and winter's harsh freeze had lifted from the heavily wooded township. The day brought forth the promise of a thriving new year, and as Stephanie awoke to the sound of whippoorwills singing nearby; she could hear the cry of loons in the far distance as well. She lay in her bed wrapped in blankets warding off the cool morning chill as a gentle breeze flowed through white lace curtains that hung above her opened window. Stephanie felt serene under her warm blankets. It was a Saturday morning, and for her that meant sleeping in. She was sure there would be no hurry to get out of bed.

All at once, Stephanie remembered it was her birthday and the idea of getting out of bed suddenly motivated her. She wondered what the day might bring and if her parents were planning something special for her. Every year, her parents had always thrown her a birthday party. Now that she was turning eighteen, she wondered if the birthdays would be the same. *This will be a good day,* she thought, and then got down upon her knees to pray.

Stephanie's prayer did nothing to stop a small bird from flying in her window and landing on the windowsill. She heard it fly in, but kept her eyes closed to give thanks to the Lord. Then the bird rudely called out, "Chic-a-de-de-de!" Stephanie smiled with delight as she recognized the unmistakable sound of Maine's state bird. Hearing that chickadee reminded her of Psalm 100:2, *Serve the Lord with gladness: come before his presence with singing,* and with this, she rejoiced.

Outside Stephanie's window was the familiar noise of a neighbor's farm tractor. As she finished praying, she looked up and saw that the bird was gone. Her room was cold for an early spring morning. Suddenly, her warm blankets seemed to call her name. She climbed back in bed, only for a moment to warm up.

Next to Stephanie's bed was a nightstand and atop of that her digital alarm clock. She was surprised to see that it was ten thirty. The house was quiet, which seemed odd, and as she sat up in bed to reach for her favorite terrycloth bathrobe, she began to realize that her parents might have gone into town. The idea that her family had gone anywhere without her made her glad because she knew they trusted her, and this day was special because she knew she was now considered an adult.

As she slipped into her bathrobe, Stephanie recalled the memory of her grandmother who had handmade the robe about a year before she died. It reminded her of the love Grammy Gallagher had for everyone. For Stephanie, the bathrobe was more than just a garment to keep warm. It was something she wanted to keep forever. For nearly two years, she had worn it faithfully because it held a special place in her heart.

As Stephanie pushed the blankets away to get out of bed, she slipped her arms through the sleeves of her bathrobe. She turned and laughed as she saw her reflection in her dresser mirror. She knew she looked amusing because her hair was wet when she had gone to bed the night before, and it had dried like cowlicks on mousse. Her beautiful long brown hair looked more like something of a rag doll. She laughed as it stood up carelessly in every possible direction. "What a mess I am," she mumbled.

Stephanie opened the door to her room and stepped into the hallway, listening carefully to see if anyone was home. The house was quiet, and all she could hear was the sound of the old wooden floors creaking as she walked slowly down the hall. The railings that bordered a second floor balcony led to the staircase, which went down into a large family room below. This was the room where Stephanie had been born eighteen years earlier. Cathedral ceilings gave the old farmhouse a majestic look.

"Hello?" Stephanie called out. "Is anybody home?"

There was no reply.

"Hello?" Slowly, she walked down the stairs.

"Mom... Dad, is anybody home?" Downstairs, she checked every room. There was nobody.

In the family room, there was a large picture window where she could see that her parents' vehicles were parked outside. She dismissed all worries.

Stephanie stepped outside on the front porch where she could see across the lake. Tiny waves of water sparkled as diamonds glistening upon glass. She could feel the touch of a cool breeze gently kiss goose bumps upon her skin. The sun's rays were warm, yet not enough to take the chill out of the air. It was a beautiful day, and Stephanie felt as though it was for her.

An hour passed by, and it seemed odd to Stephanie that her parents had not yet returned. They always left her a note telling her where they were going. In her mind, she wanted to believe they went out shopping for a birthday party. Yet, in her heart, she was starting to wonder if everything was okay. There had always been someone around to greet her on her birthday, but this day seemed different. Curiously, she walked back into the house, and in through the kitchen. On the refrigerator door was a handwritten note she had not noticed before. It read:

> Happy "Eighteenth" Birthday, Honey. We are down back fixing up the picnic area. We love you, Mom and Dad.

Just then, Stephanie heard the sound of a car coming up the driveway. She looked outside through the living room window and watched as the car made its way up past two acres of well-groomed landscaping. Hedgerows complimented flower gardens and made a very attractive setting. As the vehicle came into view, Stephanie realized it was one of the company cars from her father's business. It was Alan. She was glad to see him. He had always been the silent partner in their organization, but was close to her family since he was her father's best friend.

Stephanie watched carefully as the car pulled up along the front of the house. Curiously, she wondered what he was doing there. It seemed odd that Alan would come to the house in a company car on a Saturday. *Maybe something bad has happened?* she thought. Something did not feel right to her.

As the car stopped, she could see through the tinted windows. Alan was not alone. She wondered who was riding in the car with him. *This can't be good,* she thought, *Where's Mom and Dad?* She had a bad feeling about the situation. Stephanie was never one to rely on *feelings,* yet something did not seem right to her. As the car stopped, both front doors opened. She watched carefully through the picture window. *Could it be Mom or Dad?*

On the driver's side of the car was Alan, and the other side was the silhouette of someone she could not see. It did not look like either one of her parents. Just then, the passenger of the car emerged. It was none other than Russell, the man who she nearly knocked unconscious with a coffee pot a year ago. Stephanie was surprised to see him there. Russell had never been to the house before, and now there he was standing outside her home. She wondered why Alan would bring him to the house. The memory of Russell was something of mixed emotion. He was an attractive man, and obviously, someone she liked… after cleaning up broken glass and coffee stains. Yet, in her mind, she never thought he could be anyone who would think of her as anything more than some weird teenager. As Russell and his father stepped out of the car, she noticed he was dressed handsomely and appeared to be going somewhere important. She wondered why he was at the house, still fearing that something was wrong.

As the men walked toward the front porch, Stephanie took notice that Russell seemed better looking then he did before. He looked different to her for some reason. Standing about six feet tall and with natural good looks, Stephanie was somewhat interested to see him again. However, she was still embarrassed about the misunderstanding that had occurred a year ago. She hoped that he would not remember.

As the two men approached the front porch, she knew this would be her opportunity to make a good impression on Russell. Through the stained glass windows of the front door, she could distinguish Russell's blonde hair and husky physique standing next to Alan. Stephanie stood anxiously on the other side waiting for their knock.

Then, a knock on the door sounded. She took a deep breath and reached for the doorknob. Thoughts of what to say to them ran through her mind. She wondered what they had to say to her. Just as she was about to turn the doorknob, she remembered just how bad she looked when she climbed out of bed an hour ago. She had not dressed or done anything to her hair. She stood there in a brief panic, and then she looked down to confirm she was still wearing satin pajamas, and a terry cloth bathrobe. In a mirror across the room, she turned to see the reflection of her hair looking more like cowlicks on mousse. *Oh!* she thought, *I can't let him see me like this!*

There was a second knock on the door. She could hear the men talking outside. They sounded happy about something. This relieved her of worry that they had bad news. However, Stephanie was in a panic. She ran as fast as she could up the stairs and into her room, scurrying to get dressed. From her bedroom, she could hear the men knock on the door again, only this time a lot louder. Combs and hairbrushes flew as Stephanie rushed to make herself look better. She reached for the nearest water bottle and sprayed water on her tangled hair. She was afraid that Russell and his father would leave before she could be ready.

The knocks continued downstairs at the front door.

Too close! she thought.

Within minutes, the knocking stopped. She looked out her bedroom window in fear that Russell and his dad were preparing to leave.

From a back window in the upstairs hallway, Stephanie could see out into the backyard. Her parents were walking up to greet Alan and Russell. Relieved, she focused on getting dressed.

Moments later, Stephanie could hear the voices of her father and Alan as they entered the house. The three men were downstairs in the family room talking. Stephanie wanted to go down and visit, but was nervous about giving them the impression that she only wanted to see Russell. Still, curiously, she pondered why Alan would bring Russell to the house. She wandered down the stairs nonchalantly in an attempt to look like she was just passing through. As she entered the living room, she smiled in a way that was hiding her embarrassment. "Hello," she said.

Russell, Alan, and her father looked up at her.

"Hi," Alan said.

Russell sat quietly.

"Good morning," her father said.

"Morning," she replied. Her hair looked much better, and she felt good about herself being dressed in something other than pajamas. She took a quick glimpse of Russell. He was sitting on the couch looking at her. He smiled. It made her feel good to think that he had noticed her. "Hi," she said.

"How are you?" Russell asked.

"Good," she said with a smile.

"Have you been throwing any more coffee pots?" he jokingly asked.

Stephanie was afraid he would bring that up. She laughed. "I only throw things at strangers," she said and then continued through the family room and into the kitchen. She was happy that she had a chance to speak with Russell. She knew there was something about him she liked. Yet, she was not certain what it was. He intrigued her, and that was all she knew. His presence captured her imagination, and if nothing else, she knew she enjoyed having words with him no matter how small.

Moments later, Stephanie's mother, Melva, came into the kitchen from the outside back door. Her hands were dirty from gardening, and she saw Stephanie sitting at the kitchen table alone. "Happy birthday, dear," she said and then walked over to kiss Stephanie on the forehead. "How was your sleep?"

"Fine," Stephanie responded, trying to hide her excitement.

"Have you had breakfast yet?"

"No."

"Why don't you hold off?" her mother suggested. "Your father's going to be barbecuing down back."

Then Stephanie remembered the note that hung on the refrigerator. It was still there. She looked at her mother. "Did you accomplish what you set out to do this morning?" she asked.

"Yes," her mother replied.

There was a brief pause between the two. From the other room, Stephanie could hear her father laughing about something with Alan and his son.

Stephanie asked her mother, "What's Russell doing here?"

"From what I gather," her mother said, "your father and Alan are going to look at a new job site later today, and Russell's got some involvement with it."

Stephanie looked at her mother. "Do you think he's single?" she asked.

Her mother chuckled. "I think he's a little too old for you," she replied.

"Oh."

Melva looked at her daughter and gave her a smile. "I believe he is single," she said.

Stephanie nodded her head as if trying not to show interest. "I see," she said.

Just then, a van drove up the driveway. Stephanie could hear it pull up next to the house.

"Are you expecting company?" Stephanie asked.

"Maybe," her mother said.

There were voices coming from outside. Stephanie looked at the clock on the stove in the kitchen. It was about noon. She stood up from her chair in the kitchen and looked out the picture window. It was her best friend, Cheryl, along with a couple other friends from school. They were walking up toward the front porch and to the front door. Stephanie could see they were carrying wrapped packages. She smiled and got up to greet them at the door.

As Stephanie walked through the family room again, she glanced down at Russell as he slouched comfortably in an old futon. Then she looked away from him toward the front door.

thing, and probably something she realized that only she was noticing. Yet, she felt slightly like just one of the kids. For her, she had hoped that the opportunity to talk with Russell might be better. However, she did not let it bother her. It was, after all, her eighteenth year birthday, and she wanted to enjoy all she could. Just for fun, in her mind, her birthday wish was to get to know Russell more.

Paul started right in on cooking, and Melva helped organize paper plates, napkins, and cups. Within a short while, the food was ready.

"Let's gather around for prayer," Paul announced. Everyone stood up in a circle around the picnic table. This was somewhat traditional in the Gallagher style. Paul asked the blessing and gave thanks to the Lord.

The group had a good time. Although Stephanie's parents seemed busy with the other adults, she kept a watchful eye on Russell. Occasionally, she noticed he would glance at her. He would smile with appreciation, and she wondered if it were more for the barbecue or because he liked her. She hoped it was because he liked her, and that was enough for Stephanie to feel happy about the day.

After lunch, Melva had noticed Stephanie could not keep her eyes off Russell. She made eye contact with Stephanie from across the table, as if to say, "Be good." Melva knew her daughter well, and Stephanie did her best to behave. Paul served cake and ice cream. Stephanie opened gifts, and showed her gratitude. Mostly, she was grateful for the company she had at her birthday party.

Two hours had passed, and the small group was starting to wind down. As people got up from their chairs, Stephanie watched Russell stand up. She admired his reserved demeanor and liked everything about him. It almost seemed sad to her that he would be leaving soon without having the opportunity to talk with him more. Her friends ventured up the path to the house as she lingered with her parents to see if they needed any help putting things away. Her father spoke up. "Don't worry about things," he said. "Your mother and I will come back down and take care of this later."

As people began to leave, Stephanie knew she needed to say goodbye to everyone. She quickly started to walk toward the path to catch up. Then, to her surprise, she noticed Russell start toward the path at about the same time. She slowed down to walk with him.

"Thanks for coming," she said.

"You're welcome," he replied, and then said, "Happy Birthday."

"Thanks!"

She was glad she finally had the chance to talk with him. Oddly, she found herself walking up the path alone with him. It reminded her of the last time she was alone with him when she nearly knocked him out with a coffee pot. She was tempted to bring up the bad memory of their first meeting just for laughs, yet searched for something else better to talk about in the few moments that they had.

"So, what do you do for work?" she asked.

"Oh, I remodel old homes," he said.

"That's interesting," she replied, not really knowing what to say next. "How long have you been doing that?" she asked, just searching for anything to hold his interest.

"I've been doing that for about five years," he said. "I always wanted to have my own business. It was my dad who got me involved with building things."

"Me too," she said.

"You build things?" Russell asked.

Stephanie laughed. “No,” she said. “I mean, I want to have my own business… someday.”

“Well, that’s great,” Russell said.

As Paul and Melva headed up the path, Stephanie could hear their voices. Before she knew it, they were all back at the house. Stephanie said goodbye to her friends, and thanked everyone for coming before they drove away. Russell and Alan stayed only a few minutes later and then got in their car.

Stephanie gave Russell a smile. “Thanks, again for coming,” she said.

“You’re welcome,” he replied. “I’ll see you again sometime, I’m sure.”

She smiled at Russell. “That would be great.”

Church on Sundays

The Gallaghers regularly attended church, which was located about three miles across town from Belgrade Village. For nearly twenty years, this was the place where Pastor James ministered to a relatively small congregation. Not much had changed in the area since the mid-1800s when the building was originally constructed. The small church was one of the first structures built in the community.

Stephanie typically sat with her parents in the front left row, where the morning sun would shine brightly through the tall double hung windows that faced an easterly direction. The paved parking was one of many improvements that took place in recent years. There was also a church annex added to the building to accommodate church suppers and various other events. The kitchen had all new appliances and modern conveniences. Inside the sanctuary, there were padded pews covered in rose-colored fabric, complimented by embroidered lace curtains that hung above the clear exterior windows. The walls smelled of fresh paint, as the bright color of pale pink hues illuminated the room with the morning sun's glow. Flat cathedral ceilings painted in white curved downward to make a seemingly endless wall on both sides of the room. Wood trim stained in dark walnut gave things a finished look, while a small balcony overlooked the small stage area in the front. Along each side of the pulpit, two painted murals portraying Jesus conveniently filled window frames where the view outside was lost with an addition of the annex built in the back. One painting depicted Jesus ministering to children and another as a shepherd with His sheep. Above the pulpit, in the center of the wall was a wooden cross that had been fashioned from the original front doors that swung open for generations as clergymen from the past made their way into the sanctuary. This had been a gift to the church from Pastor James' wife, Carrie, as she suggested recycling the old doors to retain some of the building's original nostalgia. Other modern conveniences included a sound system, a video display unit, and a motorized projection screen that would drop down from the ceiling at the touch of a button. This was a very comfortable place for worship, and the people who attended loved the fellowship they shared.

Just down the road were the Bradburys, who owned the farm that sat on top of the hill overlooking the small country church. Below, fields stretched for miles running along a newly paved road fenced off by barbed wire, and a barn stood at the four-way corner called Metcalf Junction. The barn, which was owned by the Bradburys, housed several small horses, heifers, and a mule. It was this landmark that people often referred to when giving directions to the small church, which was just two hundred yards away nestled among pine trees. Many great talents had passed through over the years, as the small country church became like a bright shining star within the Belgrade community.

During certain times of the year, the pastures that surrounded the church were some of the most beautiful anyone had ever seen.

Green grass grew in the spring like a rich tapestry of finely woven second crop hay. Snow followed in the winter months as blankets of snow artfully covered the hills as the smooth contours of the land stood out like large dunes in a desert. It was a land of deeply rich soil and made for great sliding in the winter. Most common, were the Sunday afternoon youth group meetings that segued into outdoor events, where the youth appreciated the smooth hills. The Bradbury family, for generations, cordially allowed church folks to use their fields for sliding. There were many occasions when Mr. Bradbury would even rig up his sleigh and offer rides to the kids while Mrs. Bradbury kept folks warm inside, usually over a pot of hot cocoa simmering on a woodstove.

The church congregation consisted of only fifty-three people; however, the fellowship that they shared was precious. In recent years, the number of those in attendance increased dramatically with the introduction of a music program and group who frequently performed hymns in and around the central Maine area. On Sunday mornings, the parking lot would fill with cars and trucks as people crowded in from neighboring towns to hear God's Word. It was hard to believe the church roster listed so few members. Most in attendance were simply friends and relatives of existing church members that had invited them. It was a good program, and the sermons from Pastor James were always compelling. People consistently came back week after week.

Stephanie was a youth group leader and a Sunday school teacher for kids ages five and six. Her father Paul was a Sunday school teacher for the adult class, and her mother Melva played piano occasionally on Sunday evenings when there were fewer people in attendance.

It was the first Sunday in May when Stephanie recalled her unexpected surprise. The day started like any other day as she got out of bed to have breakfast with her parents. Her mother was downstairs in the kitchen cooking, as the smoky aroma of sizzling bacon and eggs worked its way up into Stephanie's room.

"Breakfast is almost ready!" her mother called from the bottom of the stairwell.

Right on cue... Stephanie thought as she looked at her alarm clock. "Be right down," she replied.

"Hey, darling," he said to his daughter. "Did you get much sleep?"

Stephanie was rubbing her eyes. "Yes," she said.

Outside the window from where Stephanie was standing, the sun shone brightly through pine trees that stood tall. There was not a cloud in sight as Stephanie looked out to admire the splendor of a clear blue sky across the Belgrade Lake.

"It's supposed to get really warm today," her father said.

Stephanie looked out into the yard. "It's pretty when the trees begin to bloom," she said.

Paul humored, "Enjoy it while you can before the black flies come."

From the kitchen, the sound of dishes clanked as Melva set the table. "Breakfast!" she called out. Stephanie and her father joined in.

The ride to church that morning was pleasant. Stephanie rode in the backseat alone as she always had. Her father drove as her mother talked of an upcoming Sunshine Committee meeting. It had been a week since her eighteenth birthday, and the memory of Russell was still fresh on her mind. Thinking about him made her heart skip a beat. She had thought about him all week during school. High school graduation was less than seven weeks away, and she wondered if she might have the chance to see him again before then. Just for fun, she humored herself by the thought of him attending her graduation. She knew if she invited Alan, his father, maybe Russell would attend. It was a fun thought. She looked down in the seat next to her, where her Sunday school materials sat, and thought of her class ahead of her that day. She was prepared, and spiritually ready, for all the day had to offer. At least, she *thought* she was.

Shortly after Stephanie arrived at the church with her parents, she thought it was odd that her father suddenly needed to go in through the rear annex. "You two go on without me, I'll meet you in there," he said.

Stephanie dismissed her father's strange behavior and went to the front of the building through the front doors.

Sunday school classes took place in both the sanctuary and annex part of the building and then finished at 10:15 a.m. after the second bell would ring. Pastor James would then dismiss all groups in prayer, and prepare for morning service.

Stephanie gathered her Sunday school materials as the few small children in her class left to meet with their parents. The room suddenly became noisy by the sound of people coming in through the building. This was a very busy time of the morning as musicians came in with their instruments and began to tune-up. A member of the music group then switched on the sound system, and hymns of praise rang throughout the building.

People continued to crowd into the sanctuary while greeting each other. There were cordial smiles and great fellowship while others stood respectfully in the pews to sing along with the music group performing in the front. Stephanie looked around for her parents but did not see them. She moved from her small classroom corner to one of the empty pews where her parents typically sat. She looked around the room and still did not see her parents. However, she knew she would see them soon. She stood in place and began singing with the group as they sang

"How Great Thou Art," reading the words as they were displayed above the cross on the overhead projector.

The prelude of music typically lasted about ten minutes while people gathered in. Stephanie began to get concerned when Pastor James entered the room and her parents were still not around. The music group began their song of praise, "Blessed Be the Name," and Stephanie continued along singing.

As the music group's song ended, Pastor James stood up to the podium and said, "Good morning." That was often his polite way of asking people to sit down. This day brought an unusually large number in because of the nice weather. Pastor James smiled with a warm welcome to all those that came in. As he began to read the day's bulletin, Stephanie continued to look for her parents. From a nearby window, she could see her mother's red Volvo sitting in the parking lot where her father left it. They were obviously still out back in the annex, but it confused her why they were tardy for morning service.

Then Pastor James spoke, asking everyone to join in singing "Faith of Our Fathers." Most people stood while they sang. Others, for health reasons, remained seated. By this time, Stephanie was having a difficult time concentrating because she was wondering why her parents were still not with her in the pew.

Just then, the door connecting the sanctuary with the annex opened. At last, it was Stephanie's parents. She could see they were both smiling. She stood singing as if nothing bothered her. As they made their way down the aisle, Stephanie moved over toward her left to give them plenty of room in the pew. They stood next to her, reaching for an available hymnal and followed along in the singing.

When the song ended, Pastor James stood in the pulpit and opened with prayer. He prayed for those who could not be there and for those with certain needs. He asked a special blessing for lost souls and that people might come to know God's love through Jesus Christ and the Holy Spirit. The congregation joined with him in reciting the Lord's Prayer, and then in traditional form, people greeted one another from their pews.

It felt like a good day to Stephanie, but she wondered why her parents took so long getting to their seats. As people moved about the sanctuary greeting one another, she asked her mother quietly, "How come it took you and Dad so long to get out here?"

Melva smiled. "Oh, your father is up to something," she said.

Stephanie wondered what her father was doing.

As the congregation slowly made their way back to their seats, Pastor James stood patiently and waited for people to settle down. He smiled, and then leaned close to the tiny foam covered microphone that stretched upward from the podium. Rather than say something, he tapped on the microphone gently, just enough to send a mild thumping sound through the small speakers that hung from the adjoining walls. He quickly had everyone's attention, and people politely sat down.

About fifteen minutes into the service, everything would have appeared normal... until Pastor James asked the deacons to come forward. Stephanie thought this was rather peculiar, and wondered if perhaps her parents' strange behavior had something to do with it. As her parents stood up to join the deacons, Pastor James said, "We'd like to recognize someone for their talents."

Immediately, Stephanie could feel the blood rushing up the back of her neck. She sat alone in her seat hoping it was not her that was about to be recognized. Stephanie enjoyed her work and service to the Lord; however, she was not one who liked to receive attention for it, nor was standing before crowds one of her favorite things to do. She feared that if Pastor James was planning to recognize her for anything that he might ask her to come forward. This was her dreaded fear.

As she watched her parents join with the deacons down front, Pastor James looked directly at her and smiled. Her stomach started to churn as she slowly crouched down into her seat. *This was a good day…* she thought humorously. As she looked over to her right, she saw a couple of people looking at her as though they knew what was to follow.

Then, Pastor James began making a speech. "Every once in a while, it's important to recognize someone who shows outstanding dedication and has given their all to the church," he said.

Stephanie sat quietly, wishfully thinking the event might be for someone else.

Pastor James continued, "We have a young woman who will be graduating from high school soon… "

That was all Stephanie needed to hear. She suddenly knew it was her that was about to get the attention. To her, it felt more like a public lynching. She thought about Pastor James' words as she looked around the room to see if she was the *only* person present who would be graduating from high school. She knew it was the church's way of giving her warm wishes.

Pastor James continued with his speech. The next words she heard were, "Stephanie Gallagher, would you please come forward?"

Stephanie smiled and showed good spirit. However, in her mind, she was thinking, *Oh, no, here we go.*

All eyes were upon her. Stephanie stood up and slowly made her way down the aisle. She nervously clinched her fingers tightly as she tried to hide her fear. She stood front and center before a full house of people. Pastor James resumed his speech. She was hot with embarrassment and felt the sweat roll off her forehead. She enjoyed being among crowds, but not the center of one. She looked up at Pastor James as he smiled. This *was* exciting for her, yet a little uncomfortable.

"Stephanie," he said. "In light of your dedication and service to the church, it was decided to recognize you for your talents and for your contributions. For many years now, you have served the Lord in ways we all can appreciate. You've helped out with cooking, cleaning, and are doing a fine job in your ministry as a youth group leader."

"Thank you," she replied in a small tiny voice.

Pastor James reached beneath the podium and held up a wall plaque for all to see. "As a token of our appreciation, we would like to present this plaque to you for all to see in hopes that you might display it for others to know how very much you mean to our church." Then, he handed the plaque down to one of the deacons, who in turn gave it to Stephanie. The congregation began to applaud. She held it in her hands and read it. When she turned around to hold it up for all to see, she looked surprised to see a standing ovation in honor of her. It was a humbling experience, and one she knew she would remember for years to come.

She smiled and said, "Thank you, everybody."

Just when she thought it was over, Pastor James said, "And knowing that your high school graduation is right around the corner, we wanted to give you something special as you embark on your journey through life."

One of the deacons came forward with a beautiful plant. It was a geranium with purple flowers and leaves having many lobes. Attached to it was a package of long bill-shaped seeds for her to plant. Pastor James said, "As a token of our appreciation, we'd like to give you this as a symbol for all the seeds that you have planted within our church, and may God bless you and continue to bless those whose lives you touch."

Stephanie did not know what to say. It was joyful to be recognized, and she felt happy. She acknowledged how nice it was for what the church had done. “Thank you,” she said, turning to Pastor James and the deacons. Then she turned around and thanked the congregation again, and as they applauded. Her smile showed an overwhelming gratitude.

On the way back to her seat, her parents joined her. As she sat down, she kept the plaque next to her and held the geranium in her hands. Frequently, she looked down at the plant as if to enjoy the fragrance, though it offered no aroma. Coincidentally, Pastor James’ sermon came from the book of Ephesians, and he talked of the importance of giving thanks. Stephanie listened closely to his words, and it was almost as if the Word of the Lord was speaking to her. She felt something in the pastor’s sermon that seemed directed toward her.

After the service, Pastor James gave his traditional benediction and wished everyone a good day. The pastor and his wife, Carrie, stood next to the entrance as people slowly made their way out of the sanctuary. They shook hands with everyone that passed by and thanked them for coming. Stephanie walked out with her father and mother, and thanked Pastor James again for recognizing her.

Pastor James said, “Thank you, young lady, for being there for us.”

“You’re welcome,” she said.

As Stephanie and her parents walked down the front steps, they made their way back to her mother’s car. Her father asked, “Would either of you like to drive?”

Melva replied, “No, I’m all set.”

Stephanie, still holding her flowers and wall plaque said, “I’m good.”

“Okay,” Paul said. “I guess I’ll drive.”

On the ride home, Paul mentioned how nice the service was.

Melva mentioned it would have been nice if Alan could have been there to see it.

"Yeah, but Alan's never been one for church," he said. "It's unfortunate."

Stephanie remained quiet for the ride home. She admired her new wall plaque as it sat in the back seat next to her, and in her lap was the geranium, which represented the seeds she had planted for the Lord. She already had ideas where she wanted to hang the plant at home. She thought it would look great downstairs in the kitchen, where it could get plenty of sunshine. Again, she thought more about Pastor James' sermon, and she remembered the words from Ephesians 5:20, *Giving thanks always for all things unto God and the Father in the name of our Lord Jesus Christ.*

What the church did meant a lot to her, and it inspired her to minister to others as opportunities might arise. Mostly, she thought of Russell and wondered if he knew the Lord. This was something she was determined to find out.

Alan Meets Edna

Edna was a widowed grandmother and a woman whom many respected in the church. Paul, Melva, and Stephanie knew her well because it was about two years earlier when Edna inherited her grandson "Steve" after his parents died in a plane crash. Steve's mother was Edna's only daughter, and it was on that tragic weekend when Steve's parents said "goodbye" to him that they never returned. Steve was staying at his grandmother's house at the time of the crash, and he had been with her ever since.

When the news of Edna and Steve's loss quickly spread throughout the community, the church responded by offering all the love and support they could with open arms. Edna already knew Jesus as her personal Lord and Savior; however, it had been many years since she attended church. Her husband had passed away about ten years earlier, and without him, she lacked the motivation to attend services on a regular basis. Having Steve in her life helped her realize that she had new reasons to strengthen her relationship with God and to ensure Steve knew of God's love, that there *is* an eternal God, as one person… Father, Son, and Holy Spirit.

As Edna started coming to church on a regular basis, Steve found he also enjoyed the services offered. Both became involved with Sunday school, Vacation Bible School, and with nearly every other ministry offered at the church.

It happened one day when Alan was out scouting for a good place to fish. Every spring, he and Russell would plan a fishing trip together. Quite often, they enjoyed traveling to northern Maine where they would rent a camp for a week, sometimes two. However, Alan was getting older and the thought of staying "local" sounded better to him every year. Belgrade Lake, after all, offered some of the best fishing around.

Just by chance, Alan drove along the back roads of Wilson Pond when he found a small dirt road wide enough for only one car at a time to pass through. At first glance, he assumed it was a private road. Then he noticed a corner street sign posted, naming it "Wilson Pond Road." He turned onto the desolate looking road thinking it might be a waste of his time. Mud puddles filled with water as the snow from a nearby grassy embankment melted in the afternoon sun. To the left, and in the direction of the lake, trees blocked the view from seeing any waterfront property. There were no houses in sight, and Alan was sure this was more of a camp road for summer vacationers. As he continued along, he considered turning around and going back as the ruts became deeper, scraping along the bottom of his car. This hardly seemed worthwhile to him. Still, just because he was a man who never liked to leave anything unfinished, he figured he would continue just to find out where the road would lead.

After traveling through roughly a quarter mile of rocks, slush, and mud, Alan was pleasantly surprised to find a quaint little house that appeared to be unoccupied. It looked as though someone had built a place in the perfect spot for hunting, fishing, and camping. He could not believe his eyes. There was a "For Sale by Owner" sign in the front yard and a telephone number to inquire. Although he was not in the market to buy a second home or camp, he was intrigued by all the features this place had to offer. As he drove up the small driveway, it quickly became apparent that someone had been there fairly recently. Tire tracks from another vehicle were in the mud, and it was clear someone kept up on the snow plowing during winter months. Utility wires from a nearby telephone pole ran to the house showing evidence of electrical and telephone service in the home. There was also a small television satellite dish nailed to a tree in the front yard, which was weathered, but appeared in good condition.

Almost immediately, Alan felt a connection to the small house. He acted more like a kid in a toy store as he began to imagine what the back yard would look like. He had to see it for himself. As he shut the car off and opened his door, the first thing he did was step into ankle deep mud. It was as if he hardly noticed the ground was still slushy. Quickly, he ran to the side of the house and walked along a slippery terrain that led down toward the back yard. The house rested on a hill, which made it perfect in Alan's eyes. There was almost no back yard at all. It was as if someone built a house in the middle of nowhere and left the surrounding forest untouched. Bushes and trees were thick all around, adding to the extraordinary amount of seclusion of house. Alan stood surprised by the solitude he felt while standing alone in the back yard. Instantly, he fell in love with the place. All he could hear was the rush of water as it flowed over the rocks that curved around the backside of the property and down toward the lake. It was as if he had stepped into an angler's paradise. About two hundred feet from the small house, the property sloped downward to the water's edge, which was called Wilson Pond. He walked through the thick bushes and trees to reach the water's edge, and then realized he had found a small goldmine. He was sure whoever would be selling the small house wanted a lot of money for it simply because of the location. He stood out from the trees that lined the private waterfront and admired the view across the lake. There were dozens of camps and homes that appeared to be year-around occupancy. Just then, a warm breeze tantalized Alan, and although he was sure *buying* this place was out of the question, he humored himself with the thought of, at the very least, inquiring about it.

Later that evening, Alan called the phone number posted on the "For Sale" sign.

A woman answered the phone. "Hello," she said.

Alan nervously asked, "Hi, I'm calling about the little house for sale on Wilson Pond?"

"Yes," the woman replied.

"How much are you asking for it?" he asked.

"I don't know," the woman said. "Have you seen it?"

"I saw it today. It looks like it needs some work. I love the location."

The woman introduced herself, "My name is Edna Richards. Would you like to see the inside?"

Suddenly, that named seemed to ring a bell with Alan. He vaguely remembered hearing about a woman with the last name of "Richards" who lost her daughter in a plane crash and inherited custody of her grandson. There was a pause.

"Would you like to see the house?" she asked.

"Yes," he replied. "… if that would be possible."

"Of course," she said.

They arranged to meet at the house the next day.

For Alan, meeting Edna at the house made him nervous. He was afraid that she would be asking too much money and that his visit with her would turn out to be a waste of time, both his and hers. Unsure of what price she would be asking , he had agreed to meet with her anyway…which he was starting to regret. He thought to himself that she was either a very bad businessperson or a very good one. Still, he kept his appointment.

As Alan drove into the yard, he saw her red Ford Taurus parked in the driveway. It was if he wanted to turn around and go home, pretending that he never called her in the first place. He took a deep breath and then sighed. He figured it was probably best to keep his word. She seemed like a nice person on the phone, however. Curiosity was getting the best of him.

As he got out of his car, mistakenly he walked right through the same mud puddle he had the day before. Suddenly, he heard the creaking of the front door opening. He looked up with a smile, hoping to catch a first glimpse of Edna, but the sun was shining brightly into his eyes.

"Hello," he said…trying to be neighborly.

"Hi, there," she replied. "I'm Edna."

He looked up, squinting as he walked toward the front door. "I'm Alan," he said. "That's some bright sunshine," he added.

As he got closer to the house, the sun was beyond the roofline, and he was able to see Edna. He reached out to shake her hand as she stood in the doorway. "Pleased to meet you," he said.

"Pleased to meet you," she said in return. "I'm glad you could make it."

As Alan shook Edna's hand, almost immediately he felt a connection with her. She made good eye contact with him, and he felt as though their meeting would go well. She was obviously no businessperson, and neither was he when it came to real estate.

"Thanks for meeting me," he said.

"Thank you for coming," she replied.

Edna gave Alan a complete tour of the house, which looked more like an efficiency apartment. The upstairs featured a kitchen and dining room combination to the left and a small living area to the right. Straight ahead, there was a closet built next to a bathroom, and then a stairwell led to the basement.

"My husband built this about a year before he died," she said, "which was about fifteen years ago."

"I'm sorry," Alan said.

"He never finished it, but I moved in hoping to save money and finish it myself."

Alan listened carefully to her story as they walked through the small house. He was quite impressed with the attention to detail her late husband gave each project. The house was so close to being done, he began to feel bad that Mr. Richards did not live long enough to see it get finished.

As they walked through the kitchen, Alan admired the mosaic ceramic tile that covered the countertops. The spaces between the tiles were still in need of grout, but that seemed like an easy task to Alan. Wood trim bordered the countertop edges, stained in a dark walnut color that complimented the tiles. Above, handcrafted kitchen cabinets meticulously hung in place as though the room came *after* the cabinetry. Alan stopped to admire the tiny designs etched into matching pine doors that displayed flowers and birds hand painted in magnificent detail, and varnished in a clear coat finish. Below, kitchen drawers displayed similar designs which strikingly blended in with the handles placed on each drawer. Wood trim varnished in a dark walnut color seemed to compliment the clear coated, natural looking cabinetry. Overhead, the ceilings were flat white, and the floors below were covered by cheap brown vinyl squares. Along the threshold that separated the small living area from the kitchen-dining room combination, dark green carpet covered the floor. There was a picture window facing the back yard, a small window to the right, and another small window above the kitchen sink. This was indeed a very small house, but Alan liked it.

As they made their way down the narrow stairwell, Alan was anxious to see what lay below. Immediately, he noticed the sliding glass door that led outside onto a small terrace. He was especially impressed how the room had a way of bringing the feeling of outdoors inside. There was a small futon against the wall, and the room appeared to be something that would make a great bedroom or handyman shop. It was perfect in Alan's mind.

"I'd still be living here today if my daughter and her husband hadn't passed away a couple of years ago," Edna said.

"I'm sorry to hear that," Alan replied. He was unsure about asking her any details about the accident.

"It was a plane crash," she said.

Alan was intrigued that she seemed so open to talk about her personal life. He did not know what to say. "My condolences," he said.

"It's been a tough road," she said. "But I have my grandson to keep me going. He's in school right now... ten years old."

Alan made good eye contact with her and listened with empathy. She seemed to open up more, and he nodded his head with understanding to some of the pain and grief she had endured.

"After his parents died, I figured my grandson had been through enough," Edna said. "He stayed with me here at this house while I took care of the funeral arrangements, but I couldn't see making him lose his home too. Stevie and I decided it would be best if we both lived at his parents' house. That way, he could at least have his room back and try to live a normal life."

Alan remembered reading about Edna's story in the newspapers. Somehow, he felt honored that she was so willing to share her story with him.

Edna felt an immediate connection with Alan. "Are you married?" she asked.

Her question caught Alan by surprise. He had gone to her house to inquire about buying it. Never did he imagine that his conversation would become personal. Nonetheless, he enjoyed talking with Edna. It had been years since he opened up with anyone. He was glad to answer her question. "Yes," he said. "I was married, but my wife passed away a few years ago."

"I'm sorry," she said. "It's hard losing someone. I know."

Slowly, the two made their way out the sliding glass door and around the house. Alan was supposed to be looking at the house, but he found himself as intrigued with Edna as he was with the house. It was odd to him, but a connection with Edna was definitely growing.

Up front in the driveway, Alan leaned against his car while Edna continued telling him about her life. He in turn shared pieces of his life, and how it was a struggle raising Russell without his mother.

Edna had a sudden look of disgust about her. "I'm sorry," she said. "You've been here all this time and I haven't even asked you if you'd like something to drink. Where are my manners?"

Alan smiled. "That's okay," he said. "I'm all set."

"I brought some instant coffee and cocoa if you'd like any," she said. "The microwave works. I can heat up some water."

Alan looked at his watch. "I don't want to hold you up," he said, hoping she would invite him back in.

"No, that would be fine. Steve's going to a friend's house after school because he knew I was coming here."

Alan smiled. "Okay, then. Coffee would be fine."

Inside, Alan learned more about Steve, and what a wonderful kid he was. They sat at the small kitchen table for several hours. Edna told him how she had agreed to be Steve's guardian if anything bad ever happened to his parents. Unfortunately, something bad *did* happen. She cherished the fact that her daughter had discussed the "what ifs" with her before she died. Steve was spending the weekend with his grandmother when his parents went on the trip that claimed their lives. After the accident, she became his legal guardian. It was what Steve wanted. In as much as it devastated her to leave the small house that her husband had built, financially she had no choice. Keeping two houses was too much on Edna's income. She said to Alan, "When I had moved the last item out with me and turned to lock the door for the last time, I knew it was in God's hands."

Alan was never a religious man and rarely considered God's Word. However, what Edna was telling him somehow made sense.

She said, "I shut the door, then looked up into the beautiful blue sky and said, 'Your will be done, Lord, not mine.' Then, I locked the door for the last time."

"How long ago was that?" Alan asked.

"It's been about a year and a half now," she said. "Moving into my daughter's house was strange. It took Stevie and me a while to adjust."

Alan, impressed by Edna's strength, could relate to the love and kindness she had for her family. He felt a real bond with her, and wondered of the possibility of actually buying her house after all they had shared. He sipped his coffee.

The sun was setting before they said "goodbye" that day. Alan looked at his watch. "Good grief," he said. "I shouldn't be so rude keeping you here so long."

"It's okay," Edna replied.

He could see that she had enjoyed his visit as much as he had enjoyed hers. As he got up from the kitchen table , he went over to the sink to rinse his cup.

"Oh, don't worry about that," she said. "I'll take care of it. Stevie and I are coming here this weekend anyway to do some spring cleaning."

Alan wondered how serious she was to sell the house.

"If you're still interested in buying this old place, I'm sure we can work something out," she said.

Alan replied, "Let me do a little research. Can I get back to you before the weekend?" he asked.

"That would be fine," she said. "Take your time."

Three days later, it happened. Alan called Edna and made an offer on her house that was too good to pass up. She almost dropped the phone when she heard how much he was offering her for the tiny little house.

"That's too much," she said.

Alan replied, "I'm afraid it's not. I did the research. It's fair market value."

There was a pause in Edna's voice.

"Hello?" Alan asked, thinking she had hung up on him.

"I just can't believe it," she said.

Alan explained, "Well, I wasn't in the market to buy, but I just fell in love with the place."

"Well, that's an offer I can't refuse," she said.

"Are you sure you want to sell it?" he asked.

Edna replied, "It means a lot to me to have it go to someone who will take care of it. If you still want it, you have yourself a house."

With that, they made plans to meet at the home Edna called "her grandson's," and in less than two weeks Edna and Alan had finalized the transaction.

At the closing, Alan and Edna seemed more like old-time friends rather than acquaintances who met with a mutual purpose in mind. It was uncanny when Alan got up to leave and shook Edna's hand saying, "I would be honored if you would come by to see the place sometime."

Edna had hoped she might be able to stay in contact with Alan. She had felt that she made a good friend. Alan felt the same.

"I feel like you overpaid me," she said.

"No, no, it's only fair," he replied. "I will take good care of your home."

"It's your home now," she said.

With that, Alan got up to leave.

"I would love to see what you and Russell will do with it," Edna said. "Call me anytime," she added.

"I will."

Two days after buying the home, Alan took his son, Russell, to the house. Alan referred to it as their camp, and they stayed there overnight. The little house needed some work; however, it was livable in its current condition. There were projects left undone. Russell was happy about his father's purchase. "I can do a lot of the finish work myself," Russell said.

Alan liked the idea of working on the house with his son. For years they had gone places together and worked together at Paul's of New England but never really did anything handy together personally. This small house was a new beginning for them.

Alan discussed plans to build off the back room in a manner that would not take away from the frontal appearance of the house. Both men admired the work Edna had done with flower gardens in the front of the house.

Russell had never met Edna, but it seemed the more his father spoke of her the more he began to get a sense of the kind of person she was. It became clear to him that his father thought very fondly of Edna. Russell wanted to install a fireplace, a TV with surround sound , and wooden beams across the ceiling. Alan liked Russell's ideas.

It was about a week later when Alan and Russell returned to the little house to stay an entire weekend. The previous weekend was more of a chance to get used to the little house and discuss plans to make changes. This weekend was to be one of many fishing trips that they would share for years to come.

Alan brought cooking supplies and a couple of folding chairs for outdoors. As the weekend approached, the weather forecast called for rain and light drizzle, which was perfect fishing weather. Both had planned to use the nearby stream and the lake that surrounded the area for fishing.

Saturday was just the opposite as Alan and Russell awoke to the sun shining. The two men got up from their makeshift beds to start the day. Russell slept on a cot, while his father slept on the couch.

With tackle boxes and fishing poles in hand, the two set out and walked along a path that ran upstream as it sparkled in the morning sun. Alan had no luck that day, but Russell reeled in a good size rainbow trout. They fried the fish for supper outside at the small house in a makeshift circle of rocks that Alan collected. The fire burned into the evening as the rain held back. The men gathered dried branches and twigs that lay on the ground nearby. As the sun set across the horizon, all they could see was the glow from the campfire. Alan shut off the outside lights to the small house, and the two felt as though they were a thousand miles away from nowhere. They sat for hours talking and laughing as they prepared the fish, dipped it in cornmeal, and then sizzled it in a frying pan over the open fire. The mouthwatering aroma of the fish frying was wonderful, and the two ate as they enjoyed a succulent late dinner. More than anything, it was the idea of being together as a father and son, and reminiscing of good times past and good times to come.

As the two bonded, Russell brought up one of the few memories he had of his mother. It was a subject neither one liked to speak of often because there was a lot of heartache and pain from the loss of Russell's mother. "I'll never forget Mom's cooking," he said.

Alan replied, staring into the fire. "Yeah, your mother sure could cook."

Then Russell asked, "Do you remember that time she got after me for climbing in the washing machine?"

Alan laughed, with a slight sadness in his voice. "How can I forget?" he said.

Then, there was silence.

Russell looked at his father. He could see how much his father still loved his mother. Then he tried to change the subject. "You know, this new place you got is great."

Alan seemed deep in thought about something. Russell feared his father was upset. He had wished his father might be able to move on with his life someday and be happy again. Then the thought of Edna entered his mind. He wondered if his father thought fondly enough about Edna that possibly they could become close friends. It was a subject on its own, and one that he never dared to bring up.

Alan looked at Russell and smiled. "I'm so glad I have you to keep me company," he said.

"Me too," Russell replied.

Stephanie Prepares for College

As summer welcomed the annual following of tourist and visitors to the Belgrade Lakes area, Stephanie looked forward to seeing familiar faces. However, she knew this particular summer would be her last before heading off to college. High school graduation was a special time for her, and it seemed God had answered her prayers. The University of Wisconsin in Madison, Wisconsin, had accepted her application, and arrangements were in order for her to begin classes there in the fall. For her, this was more like a new beginning. Most of her friends were planning to find full-time work locally, while others were planning to leave the area permanently. Some wanted college; others just wanted to be closer to the city.

Stephanie aspired to follow her parents' example by working in the construction field. Her plan was to work for her parents during summer months and then travel back to college each semester. It had become her life-long dream to study industrial engineering. She also hoped to one day fall in love with a man who might be right for her. She wondered how and where that might happen, yet she trusted God to guide her in making the right decisions.

Occasionally, she would think of Russell and wonder how he was doing. She wondered if there was someone special in his life, and if he knew the Lord. She prayed for him. Nearly eleven weeks had passed since she last saw Russell. She had hoped that he might try to call her after her birthday, but he never did. A couple of times she was tempted to call him but found she was too nervous to follow through. There were so many things about Russell that she adored. Yet, in her mind, she found contentment just keeping the memory of him in the back of her mind. College was more important to her at this point in life, and she knew she needed to focus on all the future had to offer since it was less than two weeks before making her big trip.

Meanwhile, the state of Maine was living up to its reputation as "vacationland." Lakes and rivers were busier than ever with boaters and anglers from all over. People passed by on skis in open waters while others romanced hand in hand walking through the small village that embraced the shore. Rivers flourished with fish, and merchants enjoyed the increased volume in business. For Stephanie, she knew she would miss her home, but looked forward to Wisconsin. At the same time, she was already yearning for the day when she could return to the place she loved so much.

It was July when her dad was at home coordinating the latest project with Alan. Stephanie was genuinely enthusiastic to hear what her father was working on. She had worked largely with her father, getting to know the business, and she was fascinated with construction. The design efforts that went into each new building were of particular interest to her. One of her father's responsibilities was inspecting each phase of construction. Paul's of New England was doing well, and business was booming. She also liked earning money. Her parents were fair to her, and promoted the idea that hard work and dedication would bring success. Stephanie had a genuine interest in starting a business of her own someday, and perhaps partner with her parents. Time would tell if this was where she really wanted to be.

Her father, Paul, was sharp in architectural design. He had a background in plumbing and electrical mastery. Alan was the financial backbone behind the business and helped it get started nearly two decades earlier. As the business blossomed into a thriving business, so did the need to hire more and more people to assist with the building. Paul's of New England was now employing nearly eighty full-time contractors year round. Stephanie shared in her father's passion. She wanted to learn how to design new architectural structures and help manage the financial aspect of business. She had been involved with going to building sites with her father and assisted in doing inspections. Learning many of the local building codes was a particular interest of hers. She also spent a great deal of time with her mother in the office taking care of clerical tasks. Together, Paul and Melva shared an equal interest in the business, and Paul was joint partners with his longtime friend, Alan. The trio was the heart of the business.

Unlike Stephanie, her father Paul had grown up in Missouri and moved to Maine after meeting Melva at a children's music camp more than two decades earlier. Paul was a young contractor at the time, hired to maintain the camp utilities during summer activities. Melva was a camp counselor who assisted young people. The two met at the camp and began a yearlong courtship. They fell in love and married a year later. Paul's enthusiasm to run a business of his own eventually attracted the interest of a Maine investor who also was interested in running a business. Together, they founded the small construction company that eventually took on the name of Paul himself. It was Paul who knew how to solicit for new customers and bid on jobs competitively. Alan was happy letting Paul handle that piece of the business. Together, they had a good balance of wisdom to make the business work, and when Melva was available, she became equally involved with the business. After giving birth to Stephanie, her assistance to the business worked out conveniently. Melva worked during the day as Stephanie attended school. Now that Stephanie was nearly grown up, Melva had time to work at the office full-time.

Stephanie's planned trip to college brought a mix of emotions. She was happy to be leaving, yet sad to leave behind the only life she had known. It also meant she would leave behind her best friend Cheryl. Stephanie thought that a mini-vacation with Cheryl would be appropriate before going away. She called her best friend, and Cheryl quickly accepted. The two began planning a trip almost immediately. Their destination of choice was Old Orchard Beach, Maine.

They had both been to Old Orchard Beach dozens of times in the past while growing up, and they both knew the area well. However, this would be their first time traveling to southern Maine alone by car. Stephanie first talked it over with her parents, and they approved in letting her use the car for a weekend. They trusted her judgment. Melva owned the shiny new Volvo and trusted her daughter to bring it back safely. She also knew Stephanie would have a backup plan in case anything went wrong. Stephanie had been driving for more than a year, and her father supported Melva's decision. Cheryl's mother also agreed that Stephanie would be safe to make the trip. Both girls were excited to go. It would be a weekend away, just the two of them... on the second week in August.

On the Friday before Stephanie and Cheryl's weekend away together, Stephanie listened to the weather forecast and it looked great for the weekend. She packed her favorite beach towel, shorts, bathing suit, suntan lotion, and all the essentials into an L.L. Bean canvas bag. Her mother stood on the front porch and watched as her daughter loaded garments for the weekend into the backseat. "Are you sure you've got everything?" her mother asked.

"Yes, Mom," Stephanie replied. She was feeling confident about herself.

"I want you to call me when you get there," Melva added with obvious parental concern.

"I will," she said.

Melva leaned against a pillar that supported the porch roof. *They grow up so fast,* she thought to herself.

As the sun set that evening, Stephanie went back into the house with her mother and enjoyed their time together.

Saturday morning came and Stephanie awoke to the sound of the hallway smoke alarm beeping as her mother was downstairs burning toast. She could hear her mother outside of her bedroom door fanning the battery operated smoke alarm, trying to get it to stop beeping. "Enough, already," her mother would say. "Enough."

Stephanie saw the sun shining as it rose out across treetops from her bedroom window. Suddenly, she recalled today was the day of her trip with Cheryl. She was excited about driving down to Old Orchard Beach. As her mother went back downstairs after silencing the smoke alarm, Stephanie got dressed and went down to have breakfast.

Stephanie walked into the kitchen and saw her mother sitting at the kitchen table enjoying coffee and nibbling burnt toast. She laughed at her mother.

"I can't believe you're eating burnt toast, Mom," Stephanie said.

Her mother humored. "I think we need a new toaster." Melva could see the excitement on her daughter's face. "This is the big day," she added.

Stephanie smiled as she reached into the food pantry for a box of cereal. "I can't wait," she said.

Within the hour, Stephanie brushed her teeth and was ready to pick up Cheryl. Both her parents stood outside on the front steps as she opened the driver's side door. As she climbed into the car, her mother reminded her to call as soon as they checked into the hotel.

"I will," she said.

Her father said, "Be sure to keep the cell phone on in case we need to reach you."

"We'll be fine," she said with assurance.

As Stephanie started the car and put it in drive, she rolled down the window to look up at her mom. "I'll see you Monday," she said. Then she reached over her left shoulder to fasten her seatbelt.

"Be careful," her mother said.

"I will." Then, she drove out of the yard.

Cheryl was ecstatic about their trip to Old Orchard Beach. Their plan was to drive to the beach first, then commute to the Sheridan Hotel in South Portland by evening. If it was not too late by the time they settled in, they had intended to walk over to the Maine Mall for dinner and then return to the hotel for a movie. The day was to be the highlight of their summer.

Cheryl was standing outside her mother's house as Stephanie drove into the yard. The two girls smiled when they saw each other. Stephanie wore a pair of dark wayfarer sunglasses as she parked the car. No sooner than she could open the door, Cheryl approached the car with her suitcase in hand. Stephanie left the car running as she stepped out. The difference in temperature was dramatic from the cool air-conditioning inside the car compared to the heat of the hot sun. There was not a cloud in the sky, and it seemed like a perfect day to go to the beach.

There was obvious excitement in Cheryl's voice as she approached the car. "I can't believe we have the whole weekend," she said.

"I know," Stephanie replied. "And they say the weather is supposed to be nice. I can't wait."

At the doorway of the house was Cheryl's mother, who had been watching the girls greet each other. Stephanie looked up and saw her standing there. "Hi, Mrs. Abrahams," she said.

"Good morning, Stephanie."

Stephanie was grateful that Cheryl was able to go on the trip. It meant a lot to her that Cheryl's mother trusted her. "Thanks for letting Cheryl go," she said.

"That's quite all right. You two have a nice time."

"We will," she said simultaneously with Cheryl. Then they looked at each other strangely and just laughed. It was as if they had rehearsed what to say and synchronized it perfectly.

Stephanie walked around the car to offer a hand with Cheryl's suitcase. "Need some help?" she asked.

"No, I think I'm all set." Then Cheryl opened the car door and put her suitcase in the back seat. "Oh, that air-conditioner feels nice," she said as a burst of cool air offered some relief from the tiny beads of sweat that had formed on her face. She closed the car door and then looked at Stephanie in anticipation.

Not a minute passed by when Stephanie said, "I guess we're all set."

Cheryl replied, "I'm ready." Then she turned to her mother and said, "Bye, Mom."

"Be safe," her mother said.

Stephanie turned to wave goodbye to Cheryl's mother. "See you later, Mrs. Abrahams."

"See you later," she replied.

Stephanie smiled at Cheryl. They had been waiting for this moment. "Well," she said, "Let our adventure begin!"

The ride to Portland took about two hours, which gave Stephanie and Cheryl plenty of time to talk. It was an exciting time for both of them. Stephanie found herself reminiscing of years gone by when she would often ride with her parents along the same stretch of highway she and Cheryl were traveling. Every year her parents drove them to places like the Maine Mall and Old Orchard Beach. Suddenly she realized she was doing it on her own, and for the first time in her life, she felt a sense of independence as though she had become an adult.

Several miles passed with few words spoken. Cheryl said to Stephanie, "You seem quiet all of a sudden."

Stephanie smiled. "Sorry," she said. "I was just reminiscing of the times my parents used to drive us places, and now here we are doing it on our own. It's great."

"Yes, it is," Cheryl said. "I'm glad we decided to do this." A moment later, she asked curiously, "Since your parents aren't here, does that mean we can play the radio as loud as we want?"

Stephanie laughed, "No," she said. "I don't want to explain to my mother that we blew the speakers out in her car. But, I've got some CDs in my backpack behind the seat if you want to go through them."

"Cool," Cheryl said, and before she could loosen her seat belt enough to reach behind the driver's seat, Cheryl was already humming the tune to a song that she knew Stephanie had. She found what she was looking for and quickly put it in the CD player. Music played softly as the girls quickly found interest in sharing memories of days gone by.

Stephanie asked, "Do you remember that time we went camping up at Moxie Falls?"

"How could I forget?" Cheryl snickered. "Wasn't that the time you dropped your lunch in the stream and it floated down the white water rapids, and all we could see were potato chips popping up everywhere?"

Stephanie laughed. "We must have been about thirteen. All I can picture is you wearing that blue trench coat because it had rained, and us trying to warn those people in the canoes to watch out for the floating ham and cheese. They must have thought we were strange."

Cheryl said, "We *were* strange back then."

Stephanie laughed. "What are you talking about? We are *still* strange," she said.

Cheryl agreed. "Hey, remember that time when your father was getting attacked by the seagulls at Old Orchard?"

Stephanie rolled with laughter. "I think it was more like my dad getting carried away with feeding the birds. Mom told him not to give them a whole loaf of bread at one time, and to throw the bread so the birds could share it. I don't know what gave him the idea to put the bread on his head."

"That was not one of your father's greatest moments," Cheryl said.

"I know," Stephanie admitted. "Now you know where I get my weirdness from."

As the car passed a sign for Brunswick, the girls knew they were about halfway there. "It won't be long, and we'll be in Portland," Stephanie said.

Cheryl changed the CD to another song and remembered something that had happened to Stephanie a long time ago. "Hey, what ever happened with that guy who kept following you around at the beach that time?"

Stephanie thought for a moment as she checked in her rear-view mirror to keep focus on her driving. "Oh, you mean that kid who got in trouble from his parents?" she asked.

"Yes."

"Wow, that was a long time ago. I never heard from him," Stephanie said. "He was going to write to me, but I think his parents told him he couldn't."

"Wasn't he like five years old?" Cheryl asked.

Stephanie giggled. "I'm not sure he was even that. Cute kid though."

"I remember he liked you a lot," Cheryl said laughing.

"Yeah, he must be in the first grade by now."

The girls laughed.

Stephanie added, "Wasn't that the day we went walking out to the island and almost couldn't get back before the tide came in?"

"No, that was Reid State Park," Cheryl said.

Stephanie suddenly remembered. "Oh, that's right. I remember my parents asking us *not* to stay out there too long. Then, we had to rush to get back in. That was creepy being ankle deep in a hundred yards of ocean water."

"I wouldn't want to do that again," Cheryl said. "What were we thinking?"

"God was watching over us that day," Stephanie murmured.

A minute of silence went by. Then Cheryl asked, "Have you seen Russell?"

Stephanie seemed surprised by Cheryl's question. She stumbled to give an immediate answer, while trying to keep her eyes on the road. "Yes," she said.

Cheryl's eyes lit up. "You have?" she asked.

"No," Stephanie said. "I mean yes, I think about him. But *no,* I haven't seen him for a while."

Cheryl could see the interest in Stephanie's eyes for Russell. "Do you like him?"

Stephanie was quick to answer. "I think about him a lot," she said.

"Why don't you call him?" Cheryl asked.

Stephanie pondered. "I think he's probably busy."

"Well, I think you should call him," Cheryl said.

"Besides," Stephanie added, "if he was interested in me, I'm sure he'd be calling *me*."

Cheryl was inquisitive. "What if he spends his days thinking the same thing about you?" she asked.

Stephanie shrugged her shoulders not knowing what to say.

Cheryl asked, "How would you describe your perfect dream guy?"

Stephanie smiled. "How would I describe my perfect dream guy?" she asked. "I don't know. What would be *your* perfect dream guy?"

Cheryl sat back in her seat dreamy-eyed, pondering the question. "I don't know," she said. "I guess I just imagine my dream guy as someone who I can grow old with, and they will always be good looking. Whoever I marry needs to be attractive."

Stephanie seemed amused by Cheryl's response. "Russell's a good looking guy."

"That's what I'm saying," Cheryl said. "You should call him."

"I might someday," Stephanie said. "I guess in my mind, the kind of guy I picture myself marrying will be someone who I can love forever for who they are. It's not all about looks. I want someone who is kind, caring, loves God, and appreciates people for who they are. That's the kind of person I want to fall in love with and marry."

Cheryl asked, "Well, don't you feel anything toward Russell?"

"I do," Stephanie said. Then she realized she said one of the most important things that she might ever say, *I do.* She went on to explain herself, "I know I miss not seeing him, and I *do* care about him. I am just not sure if he is the one God has planned for me. In my heart it is okay for me to learn more about him, but I also want God to be in control of my life, and not for *me* to overlook what He might have planned for me."

"Then you should call him before he gets away," Cheryl said persistently.

Stephanie understood Cheryl's point, but was careful not to be impulsive. She was unsure of Russell's faith and if he believed in the Lord. She said to Cheryl, "Time will tell."

The girl's eyes quickly lit up with excitement as they turned onto Ocean Drive, which led directly toward the beach. From a distance, they could see the famous Old Orchard Beach pier that stood tall for generations. There was also an amusement park on the beach, which had become a popular tourist attraction. The first ride in view was the Ferris Wheel. Stephanie warned, "You aren't getting me on that!"

Cheryl's voice expressed excitement as she noticed an ever increasing number of people walking along the streets and riding bikes. The speed limit slowed to twenty-five miles per hour as they made their way through heavily populated areas. The streets were lined with small houses and camps for rent, and it was peak season in the town of Old Orchard Beach, Maine. Everywhere the girls looked, they saw "No Vacancy" signs.

As the car rounded a corner, they suddenly saw that the beach was less than two miles away. Stephanie took a closer look at the Ferris Wheel, and said again, "There is no way I am getting on that."

Cheryl laughed. "Me neither," she said.

It was getting exciting for both of them. Up ahead, a traffic cop was directing cars. The streets were busy as a horse and buggy passed by and pedestrians crossed to a sidewalk. There was not a cloud in the sky, and it was obvious they picked a good day for the trip. As they slowly made their way toward the beach, they began scouting for a place to park. Parking lots were abundant, but most were full. Stephanie turned onto a side street, which ran along a railroad track where she found a parking lot that had vacancies. There was a man standing at the entrance to collect the fee of eight dollars. Stephanie rolled down the window to the air-conditioned Volvo, surprised by the heat that entered the car. She handed the man the money, and he directed her to an empty parking space.

They had made it. The first thing Stephanie did was call home to her mother to say they had arrived safely. Melva told her she would call Cheryl's mother to let her know they had made it down to the beach. Her mother said, "Have fun."

After parking the car, they walked along a busy sidewalk lined with vendors serving fried dough, pizza, and ice cream. Music played as they passed a game room full of video games. Cars of every kind and motorcycles passed by along the busy streets, and it seemed everyone was in good spirits. Stephanie and Cheryl stayed close together as they carefully crossed the street that led to the beach. Nearby was the amusement park, crowded with people as they lined up for various rides. The sound of The Pirate squeaked as shrills of thrill seekers screamed with excitement. A short distance away, they watched as the famous Flying Trapeze swung high overhead, as legs and feet dangled from seats high in the air. A new addition to the park was the Log Flume. Stephanie was splashed with a few drops of water as they walked past it.

Every corner of the park featured rides, games, and places to eat. What they wanted more than anything was to walk along the pier, and then relax on the beach. The pier was busy with people as they visited the various souvenir shops that had helped make Old Orchard Beach become so famous. There was an artist painting caricatures of people for just fifteen dollars. Cheryl said, "We've got to do that."

"Okay," Stephanie replied. "Let's get one made up before we leave."

Straight ahead was a man with a snake who appeared to be offering people to have their picture taken with it. Stephanie and Cheryl immediately cringed and turned the other way. At the end of the pier was a bar, and that did not interest them in the least. With so many shops, it made it difficult to see out over the ocean which something they wanted to do. Among the crowd of people making their way from one end of the pier to the other, they slowly made their way to an area on the pier that had an opening where they could see out over the beach. There were several magnifying viewfinders , and for a quarter, they were able to look out over the beach. They amused themselves by taking turns as Cheryl put a quarter in one of the machines.

"See anybody we know?" Stephanie asked.

"No," Cheryl said.

Stephanie reached into her handbag and took out her camera. She took a picture of Cheryl. Then, she stood next to her friend with her back to the ocean. Cheryl posed with Stephanie as they smiled, and Stephanie took a self-portrait of them leaning against the railing with the beach in the background. A man walking by saw Stephanie trying to steady her camera for another self-portrait. "Can I help you with that?" he asked.

Stephanie was delighted. "That would be great," she said. Then, she handed him the camera and posed with Cheryl. They stood together with their arms over each other's shoulders and the beach in the background as they smiled.

The man took their picture. "Perfect," he said, and then handed the camera back to Stephanie.

"Thank you," she said.

"You're welcome," he replied and then walked away.

Eventually, the girls made their way to the beach. There were crowds of people everywhere; however, they found an ideal little spot where they could lay out their towels and an umbrella for shade. It was about fifty feet from the water and right in the center of everything. In the distance, music played from the carousel as it gave rides to people of all ages. Children walked by with cotton candy, and Stephanie and Cheryl reached into their handbags for sunscreen.

Green ocean waves splashed into thin layers of white suds cresting across the sand and fizzling back into the Atlantic. There were hundreds of people enjoying the sand and surf along the shore, and Stephanie wondered if Russell ever liked to go to the beach.

It was about 4:00 p.m. when the girls decided to go back up on the pier to have their picture drawn by the artist they had seen. They were delighted to see he was still there. They stood in line and waited to have him draw their caricature together. Cheryl asked, "Who's going to keep this?"

Stephanie replied, "We can share it. Maybe you keep it while I'm at college, and I can have it when I come home… then, you get it back when I leave again."

"Good idea," Cheryl said.

They were next. The man helped Stephanie and Cheryl sit comfortably on a couple of chairs while he began his work. He asked, "What is it you two ladies like to do?"

Stephanie said, "I'm a Sunday school teacher."

Cheryl replied, "I'm a youth group leader at a different church."

The man worked steadily and humored the girls with silly knock-knock jokes. In less than ten minutes, he was finished. Stephanie and Cheryl anxiously waited for him to turn the easel around. When he did, they were pleasantly surprised. They laughed at the image he had made of them. Creatively, he put their cartoon caricatures before a mountain in the background with a cross appearing in the sky among a fading sunset, symbolizing God's handy work. On it, he wrote the words "Together Forever."

Stephanie and Cheryl liked the personalized touch the man gave to their drawing. They wanted to pay him the fifteen dollars advertised on his sign. As he rung up their purchase, they were surprised to see $30 appear on his florescent cash register display. They looked at each other as if he had cheated them. Cheryl reached into her bag for another fifteen dollars, and paid the man. They were a little disturbed that his sign advertised fifteen-dollar portraits, but refrained from causing a dispute. Stephanie then noticed the fine print on his sign. She quietly pointed it out to Cheryl as they were walking away. Nonetheless, they were happy with the man's artwork and enjoyed looking at the picture.

All went well as the two girls arrived in South Portland safely. Stephanie found the Sheridan Hotel without any trouble as the Maine Mall road was busy with Saturday evening shoppers. She drove into the Sheridan hotel parking lot and purposely parked her mother's car away from the crowded area hoping to avoid any unexpected dings in her mother's car. Both girls were excited to reach the hotel.

Cheryl unbuckled before the car came to a complete stop, eagerly looking out the car window at the two round hotel towers that formed the Sheridan. "This is going to be so great," she said.

The sun had settled down close to the horizon and was shining brightly from where they had parked on the westerly side of the Sheridan parking lot. It was almost blinding as the girls looked up at the hotel.

Stephanie slipped down her sunglasses to glance up at the oval-shaped, amber colored, glass architecture as it reflected the sun's rays. "Imagine what it took to build that," she said.

"Yeah, yeah, yeah… let's go inside," Cheryl said.

Stephanie sat for a moment in awe as she looked up at the building's design. She shut the car engine off.

"What part will we be staying in?" Cheryl asked.

"I'm not sure," Stephanie replied.

Cheryl cheerfully added, "It doesn't matter… We're here!"

As the two walked in through the front doors of the hotel lobby, a look of surprise was on their faces. They marveled at the terra cotta styled ceramic tiles that covered the atrium floors and glass walls separating the hotel swimming pool. Adjacent to the lobby was the hotel restaurant and concierge. This was more money than Stephanie wanted to spend, yet she knew it was a rare special occasion, and she wanted to make the trip exciting. Cheryl had agreed to pay for half of the expenses, and to them they could quickly see it was worth it. The girls checked in at the front desk and were soon on their way. With proxy cards in hand, the two girls giggled like a couple of traveling humorists as they carried their bags to the hotel elevator.

Their room was on the fifth floor. Cheryl was like a kid in a candy store. "We should go swimming later," she said.

"I agree," Stephanie replied as they walked anxiously down the hall counting room numbers on the doors passing by. When they found their room, they were enthusiastically surprised. Their room was pie-shaped due to the round construction of the building and much nicer than they had expected. Their room offered two beds and a view overlooking the Maine Mall. The clock on the nightstand displayed "6:30 p.m.." Each bed invitingly had the blankets turned down, and on one sat the hotel services card and restaurant information.

"We should order room service," Cheryl said.

"I agree," Stephanie replied. Then, she noticed some of the prices on the menu. "Maybe we should skip room service," Stephanie said.

Outside their window, the sun was fading into the distance as blue sky revealed the reflection of a jet passing by at low altitude as it took off from nearby Portland International Jetport. Stephanie used this time to call her parents to say they had made it to the hotel safely. Then Cheryl called her mother.

The evening came and went. The two girls walked across the street to the Maine Mall as planned, and everything went well. They ate supper at the mall in the food court. Some of their favorite restaurants were there set up like window service delis. Stephanie purchased a Happy Meal at McDonald's, while Cheryl came back with pizza and a taco. They enjoyed the atmosphere and their time away from home. After eating, they walked all through the mall visiting their favorite stores. Neither of them spent much money, though they had fun browsing. They walked from one end of the mall to another and stopped along the way to buy pretzels and their favorite drink, an Orange Julius. It was a good time for both of them.

As the mall closed, Stephanie and Cheryl walked outside and were surprised by the darkness that had fallen over the city. Mall patrons walked with bags and boxes as they made their way to vehicles scattered throughout a large parking lot. Stephanie and Cheryl looked at each other wondering where their hotel was. They were sure it was standing when they came to the mall. Then, they realized they had exited through a different entrance from when they originally arrived at the mall. They laughed at each other for their silliness. As they turned the corner from Sears, they saw the Sheridan hotel standing across the street. They carefully made their way back to the hotel and were in for the night. The day was all they had hoped it would be.

Stephanie awoke Sunday morning to bright sunshine that penetrated the heavy curtains that hung from the hotel window. She looked over to the bed where Cheryl had been sleeping. The bedspread hung about the bed and was partially on the floor. She could hear the shower water running. Stephanie reached into her L.L. Bean bag for the Bible that she had brought with her. She thought of the fun time she had with Cheryl the day before and began to read Psalm 50:14, *Offer unto God thanksgiving; and pay thy vows unto the most High.* She was grateful for the time she shared with Cheryl and felt a special reverence toward God.

Within the hour, the two girls checked out of the hotel, and then drove to the International House of Pancakes for brunch.

As the day ended, Stephanie and Cheryl made it back home safely. The weekend had been very good for both girls, and they knew they made memories that would last a lifetime.

Stephanie's weekend away with her best friend, Cheryl came and went. She now felt ready for college.

Stephanie Goes to College

Sunday afternoon came as Stephanie sat on the porch of her parents' home. It was hazy, hot, and humid—unusual weather for the Belgrade Lakes area during the last week in August. She sat on an old wooden rocking chair that had been on her parents' porch for as long as she could remember. It creaked as she rocked across the dried deck boards. She welcomed the scorching heat of the sun as it beat upon her legs and arms. She sat back just enough so the overhanging roofline of the porch provided her with enough shade so the sun was not in her eyes. This would be her last day in Maine before traveling to Wisconsin, so she wanted to enjoy every moment of it. She knew she would miss the area and all that came with it.

Her attention drew to a car pulling into the driveway and slowly making its way up to the house. She immediately recognized that it was Alan's car.

As he pulled up, he parked the car right in front of her, unaware that he was blocking her view across the lake. It did not matter… she was glad to see him. As he got out of the car, she noticed he seemed to be short of breath. He smiled at her, as a grandfather would for his granddaughter. "How are you doing?" he asked.

She smiled. "Great," she said.

Alan closed his car door and walked toward the steps. There was slowness in Alan's walk that she had not seen before. He sensed she noticed it, and then commented on the weather. "It's a hot day," he said.

"Yes, it is," she replied.

"This humidity really makes it difficult to breathe," he added.

There was something in his hand, and it looked like a birthday card. She wondered if it was for her.

As he walked toward the edge of the porch, he looked up at her in the chair and asked, "Are you all ready for school?"

"Yes," she said.

"Got your bags packed?"

"Yup, I do!"

Alan sat down on the edge of the porch with one leg up on the deck so he could turn to see her. She watched, as he struggled to lift his leg up onto the deck. He was tired and acted lame. It seemed his age was showing.

"Are you all right?" she asked.

"Oh, I'm fine," he said. "It's this dang muggy weather… makes it hard to breathe," he repeated.

He turned to reach up to where she was sitting and handed her the card. "This is for you," he said.

Stephanie looked at him with delight. "You didn't have to get me anything," she said.

"No, I didn't get you anything," he said. "It's just a card."

"Well, cards are gifts," she said, giving him a strange look.

Then she opened the envelope. It was a going away present. Inside, was a beautiful card wishing her the best on her trip to college, and a check for a thousand dollars.

Stephanie did not know what to say. She could not believe her eyes. "I can't accept this," she said.

Alan was quick to respond, as if he had rehearsed it many times before. "I knew you'd probably say that, which is why I already talked about it with your parents."

"But, that's too much," she said.

Alan smiled. "Listen, you deserve it. You are like the daughter I never had. You have such a bright future ahead of you, and I know you are going to make good choices in your life. It means a lot to me that you accept it, and use it for whatever you need."

"Yeah, but..." she said.

"No arguments," Alan said. "You should respect your elders."

Then Alan smiled. She could see he was up to something.

"Your father told me you were going to give me a hard time," he said. "That's why they're both watching you from that window right now."

Stephanie turned around and looked up at the windows behind her. Her parents were standing in the large picture window with smiles on their faces. They waved to Stephanie, as if to say "gotcha!" Stephanie got out of the rocking chair, and leaned down to where Alan was sitting and gave him a hug. "Thank you," she said. "I'll use this to help pay my tuition."

"Use it for whatever you'd like," he said.

The front door opened. Stephanie stood, and confronted her parents. "You knew about this?" she asked.

Paul put his arm around Melva and smiled with a big grin. "We knew," he said.

Stephanie was overwhelmed.

Melva noticed Alan seemed to be sweating profusely in the hot sun. "Won't you come inside and cool off?" she asked him.

"I'd like to, but I need to be going," he replied.

Melva knew how stubborn Alan could be at times. "Can we get you some lemonade or something?" she asked.

Alan surprisingly nodded his head. "Yes," he said. "That would be fine… lemonade would be great."

Stephanie spoke up. "I'll go get it," she said. As she opened the door to the house, she turned and asked if anyone else wanted anything.

"We're all set," her mother replied.

"Be right back then," she said.

Minutes later, the door opened, and Stephanie emerged with two tall glasses of ice-cold lemonade. She handed one to Alan as it dripped of condensation, and the other was for herself. "Thank you," he said.

"You're welcome," she replied.

They watched as Alan gulped down the eight-ounce drink as if he was dehydrated. The day was hot, but seemed to be affecting Alan more than Stephanie, or anyone else. "Can I get you some more?" Stephanie asked.

Alan swallowed the last few drops of lemonade as ice cubes rattled in the bottom of his glass. "That was delicious," he said.

"We have plenty," Melva said.

Alan looked refreshed as he set the cup on the deck. "No, thank you. I'm all set," he said. "Besides, I need to be going."

It was just minutes later, and Alan got up to leave. Stephanie, again, thanked him for his generous gift. "I'll write to you every week and tell you how things are going," she said.

Alan opened his car door. "That would be great, sweetie. You take care of yourself out there," he said.

"I will," she replied.

Stephanie stood on the porch with her parents and waved "goodbye" as Alan drove away. She wondered why he did not bring Russell.

On the day Stephanie left for Wisconsin, Paul and Melva drove her to the airport. It was a tough time emotionally. This was the first time Stephanie had ever been away from home for any length of time. Riding in her mother's Volvo reminded her of the trip she had made to South Portland and Old Orchard Beach with Cheryl. Now, returning to South Portland to board a plane seemed so different. She was nervous and had a lot to look forward to, yet at the same time, she knew she would miss her family and friends. She rode along in the back seat as they traveled down Interstate 95 and had time to reflect upon things. She kept the thought of the Lord with her, trusting He would be there for guidance. There were butterflies in her stomach, and it gave her a bellyache. She knew she would be fine because going to college was what she had dreamed of doing.

At the airport, preparing to say goodbye was difficult. The wait was nearly two hours by the time they checked in through security, and were able to sit in the waiting area. Stephanie chose a seat that was near the terminal where she was going to board the plane. They also had a great view of the arrival and departure times as they displayed on overhead video screens. Stephanie's flight tentatively was on schedule. They waited patiently as the jetport filled with people making busy connections.

Melva sat next to Stephanie. Paul sat next to Melva. Stephanie had her luggage in the other seat. They were all nervous for her.

Paul looked over at his daughter and reached across Melva to touch Stephanie's hand. "I know you're going to do great," he said.

"I'll do my best," she replied.

Melva tried reading a book to pass the time in between their conversations. Most often, she would put the book down to talk with her daughter.

About twenty minutes passed by, and things grew quiet between Stephanie and her parents. The noise in the room seemed to block out some of the anxiety they were feeling. All they could do was continue waiting for the plane to arrive. Stephanie became involved with reading some of the literature regarding Wisconsin University. It was material she had already seen, but was simply passing the time. Just then, they all heard a familiar voice that was easily recognizable. Stephanie saw a pair of familiar boots on the floor before her as she looked up. It was Russell.

Stephanie's jaw nearly hit the floor. Paul stood up to shake Russell's hand.

"Hi, son," he said to Russell.

Stephanie was intrigued that her father called Russell "son."

"What a pleasant surprise," Melva said.

Stephanie looked up at Russell in disbelief that he was standing in front of her. Russell joked, "Well, I was just passing by and happened to see you folks all sitting here… looked like you could use some company."

Melva looked at her daughter. "Look who came to see you off," she said.

Stephanie gave Russell a smile that was a mile wide. "Hi!" she said. She was amazed to see him standing there. "Wow!" she said. He smiled at her.

"I didn't want you to leave without having the chance to say goodbye, so I decided to stop in."

Stephanie still could not believe it. In her mind, this meant that he liked her. She quickly moved her luggage from the seat that was next to her. "Care to have a seat?" she asked him.

"Sure," he said and then sat down.

Melva looked over to Russell. "Is your father working today?" she asked.

"No, ma'am," he said.

Stephanie was fascinated by Russell's mannerisms. It sounded funny to her to hear him refer to her mother as "ma'am." She knew this was an open opportunity to flirt with him. She looked at Russell with a questioning expression.

"What," Russell said.

"Ma'am?" she asked.

Russell smiled. "What do you want me to call her?" he asked.

"I don't know," she said. Stephanie looked at her mother. "What should he call you, Mom?" she asked.

Melva said, "I liked ma'am."

Stephanie made a funny face. "That just sounds so weird," she said.

Just then, the customer service representative working at the counter made an announcement over the paging system that Flight 927 would be arriving at gate three. This plane would take Stephanie to Chicago, where she would board a different plane that would then fly her to Madison, Wisconsin. The time for her to leave was drawing near.

Paul looked at Stephanie with his eyes wide. "It won't be long now," he said.

The butterflies in Stephanie's stomach returned.

Russell said, "You're going to do great out there."

Stephanie suddenly remembered her father said almost the same exact thing. "I'll do my best," she said to Russell.

They watched as the plane taxied up to the gate. Paul and Melva stood up. They could see she really did not want to leave. It was obvious she had enjoyed her time spent sitting next to Russell. He stood up from the seat. Stephanie reached for her luggage and pulled out her tickets.

As they walked toward the service counter, Stephanie looked at her parents with small tears in her eyes. Melva started to cry. Paul looked at Russell as if to say something chauvinistic about women crying easily. Then, he himself started to get teary-eyed. Russell said, "You all are making me sad."

Stephanie quickly laughed. "We're fine," she told him. "That's just how we are."

They stayed together until Stephanie was next in line to enter the gate terminal. She looked at her parents and gave them each a hug.

Russell stood looking at Stephanie awkwardly. It was as if he wanted to give her a hug, but felt unsure, thinking it might not be appropriate in her parents' eyes.

After Stephanie said her "goodbyes" to her parents, she turned to Russell wondering how to thank him for coming. She looked at him as if she was expecting him to shake her hand or give her a hug... or something. Paul said to Russell, "You can hug her. She won't bite... I promise." He laughed.

With that, Stephanie and Russell gave each other a quick friendship hug. "Have a good trip," he said to her.

Then, she proceeded down the long hallway to the plane.

There was a smile on Stephanie's face as she took one last look behind her to see them all standing there waving goodbye.

Living in Madison, Wisconsin, was all Stephanie had hoped it would be. She missed Maine, but her classes kept her extremely busy. Her studies were challenging, and she tried very hard to keep up with the rigorous schedule. To help assist with tuition, she found work as a part-time server at Cleo's Mexican restaurant. For the most part, Stephanie adjusted well to life away from home. She missed the sights and sounds of Belgrade Village; however, the experience of being away for a while, she knew, would be good for her.

Madison was a completely new world from what she had grown up to know. The streets were busy with students riding scooters and mopeds, as coffee shops encompassed every end of the city. This was a very busy community, but friendly. On one side of the city was Lake Mendota, and on the other side of the city was Lake Monona. In the center was the state capitol building, and all around were neighborhoods and streets that seemed inviting. In her spare time, she enjoyed walking down along the water's edge as it reminded her of home. Being near the water was a place she found relaxing, as it reminded her of Maine and helped her with her studies. Cold Canadian winds that swept down from the north across Lake Mendota caught her by surprise from the heat wave Belgrade Lakes had just a few weeks earlier. She dressed warm and sat on park benches placed along paved walkways that passed through a beach. Joggers and cyclists frequented the area. Occasionally, she would see a couple walking along the beach hand in hand, and it reminded her fondly of Russell.

There had rarely been a dull moment since she had arrived. All of Madison seemed like one huge college campus to Stephanie. For the first time in her life, she was away from home, and it surprised her how well she was dealing with it. Possibly, it had a lot to do with there being hundreds of other students her age from all over the world. She found most of the people there to be very friendly, and she felt reasonably safe when walking around the city. Her classes were tough, but she liked her instructors and valued the school. This, she knew, would be home for her for a couple of years. However, she also knew long-term, her heart was still back in Maine. Sundays came and went, and she felt the emptiness of not being able to attend church. There were a few students she met that were devoted Christians, and they shared similar interests with Stephanie. They, too, missed the churches they had known from their hometowns. One student suggested they hold their own time of fellowship on Sunday mornings, and they did. Every Sunday, Stephanie met with her new friends and they had church service.

As Christmas season came, Stephanie returned home to Maine to spend time with her family and friends. She felt most comfortable being in her home church, and it was a special time for her as it had always been. However, the two-week stay seemed to pass by much too fast. She had hoped to see Russell during her vacation away from college, even if only for a brief moment. Yet, it seemed Russell was somehow too busy or unaware of her presence at home. She feared calling him in fear that he may have an interest in someone else. In her mind, she rationalized that *he* should be the one calling her if he was truly interested in getting to know her. It was slightly discouraging yet she did her best to stay focused on school, and her safe return to Madison, Wisconsin, went as planned.

Stephanie was proud to know she was making a difference in her life by attending college and meeting new people. It gave her a sense of self-confidence, and she admittedly liked the attention she was receiving. Like her father, she had become more assertive in the way she addressed people and learned to interact with others on a more professional level. Standing at only five feet tall and weighing just one hundred and ten pounds, she had matured into a very business oriented young woman, and for the first time in her life, she felt a sense of independence. The school year had done wonders for her intellect, and like her father, she was not afraid to speak her mind when it came to issues that she believed in.

Stephanie kept in close contact with her parents. Every Sunday night she would call them to let them know everything was all right. On Wednesdays, her mother was typically the one to call *her.* E-mail also made a great tool to stay in touch. As promised, Stephanie stayed true to her word in keeping in contact with Alan. She wrote to him every week just to say "Hi." Russell remained on her mind throughout the entire school year as well. She wondered how he was doing, and included him in her prayers.

Summer Vacation

At the end of Stephanie's first year in college, she welcomed the thought of living back in Maine. Her time away had been good, but the idea of returning home seemed inviting. She had planned to work with her parents again at their business. She had learned a lot about business management and industrial engineering. Having an opportunity to use some of those skills seemed exciting to her.

Touchdown at the Portland International Jetport was like music to Stephanie's ears. She looked out the window off the left wing as the jet screamed pass the terminal where her parents were waiting. The jet slowed to taxi, and then slowly made its way to the ramp. Stephanie did not realize how much she had missed Maine until it came to a full stop. Her stomach quivered with butterflies as she reached down for her carry on bag that was stowed beneath the seat in front of her. Passengers and crew stood waiting for the plane's door to open. Stephanie leaned forward to look out the small windows, hoping to catch a glimpse of her parents. Gray skies filled with clouds made it difficult to see anybody as it reflected off the airport terminal glass.

Stepping off the plane felt cold compared to the warmer temperatures they were having in Madison, Wisconsin, earlier that day. As Stephanie followed a line of passengers making their way up the long hallway, she started to smile in anticipation of seeing her parents. She was surprised to reach the airport's waiting area and not see them anywhere. She looked at her watch, and then checked the clocks hanging on the walls. There was a difference of one hour between Wisconsin time and Maine's time. She looked confused that her parents were not there waiting as she exited the plane. She wondered if something bad had happened. According to her mother, they were going to be there.

Just then, she heard her mother call her name. She turned and saw her parents standing at the other side of the security check in area. She smiled with joy. "Hi!" she yelled, and then ran over to greet them.

It was a bittersweet moment. She was so happy, yet had tears of joy in her eyes. Her father smiled, and they all embraced.

On the ride home, Stephanie could not stop talking. She sat in the back seat and enjoyed every mile that passed by.

Stephanie was anxious to sleep in her own bed again. "Do I still have my room?" she asked.

Her mother smiled. "Of course you do," she said.

"How are things at the office?"

"Things are great," her father replied. "We can't wait to have you back."

There was a brief moment of silence.

"Is business booming?" Stephanie asked.

"We're doing well," her father said.

Then, Stephanie started to wonder about Russell. It had been some time since she had talked about him with her parents. It seemed to her that he might have met someone and perhaps started a new life. At least, that is what she was thinking.

She was afraid to bring Russell up in the conversation so soon. "How's Alan doing?" she asked.

"He's all right," Melva replied.

"Does he still see Edna?" she asked, curiously.

"Yes," her mother said.

It was as if Melva knew where her daughter's questions were going to lead. She said to Stephanie, "I believe Alan thinks fondly of Edna. He's even started coming to church recently."

Stephanie was in disbelief. "Really?" she asked.

"Praise God," her father said.

Stephanie could not believe her ears. The news of Alan attending church was something she had prayed about many times. There was a joy in her father's voice. She could tell that Alan had finally committed himself to the Lord. It seemed one of her prayers had been answered. "Wow," Stephanie said. "That's great."

There was a pause. Stephanie asked, "How's Pastor James doing?"

"Oh, he's doing fine," her mother said.

"How's Carrie?"

"She's well."

Stephanie really wanted to ask about Russell, but was in fear of hearing he had met someone and moved on with his life. "How's my geranium?" she asked.

There was silence.

"Why don't you ask about Russell?" her mother asked.

Stephanie was suddenly speechless. Her mother's question caught her by surprise. For nearly a year, Russell had remained on her mind. Hearing her mother mention his name made her heart skip a beat. "How *is* Russell doing?" she asked.

"He's doing great," her mother said. "He plans to take over for his father when he retires."

Stephanie joked, "When Russell retires?"

"No, silly, when Alan retires," her mother said. "He's been helping us out with remodeling. Plus, your father's had him at some of the different job sites for inspections."

Stephanie's father said, "He's quite an individual, that Russell."

Stephanie wondered if her father said that for any particular reason. He seemed anxious to talk about Russell, as if he knew Stephanie wanted to know everything Russell had been doing for the past year. She wondered if Russell was seeing anybody socially. "Is he married?" she asked.

Her mother laughed. "Heavens, no," she said. "He's too busy for that."

Her father added, "I'm not sure that boy's ever going to get married."

Stephanie sat in the back seat confused by her parents' comments. "How come you don't think Russell will ever get married?" she asked.

"He's a busy boy," her father said. "Maybe, someday with the right person he might settle down."

Stephanie was a little glad to hear him say that.

Then Melva said something that made Stephanie happy. "He's always asking about you," she said.

Stephanie's eyes lit up with joy. "Really?" she asked.

"It's pretty clear he likes you," her mother said. "Haven't you two kept in touch?"

"Well, no," Stephanie said. "I didn't think he would have any interest in someone gone away to college for a year at a time. He's got his own business, and I didn't want to be in his way."

Her mother spoke in a way to boost Stephanie's self-esteem. "I am sure he would be delighted to hear from you." It was as if she knew Russell's thoughts.

Stephanie felt good inside at her mother's comments. She sat back in the seat, thrilled by the news that Russell had been asking about her. She watched as her father took his eyes off the road briefly, just long enough to look at her mother. He smiled as if he knew a secret. Melva smiled back at him. It was as if they were both conspiring to surprise Stephanie with something. She began to wonder. Then, she thought of the possibility that Russell might be waiting at the house for them when they arrived home.

He was not.

Days later, Stephanie was at home and settled in. She was happy to sleep in her own bed again and to have her own room back. Her parents' home cooking was also a treat.

Sunday came, and it seemed the church had planned a small homecoming welcome for Stephanie. She sat proudly as Pastor James stood from the pulpit and announced how great it was to have Stephanie back. She sat elated by the gesture, unlike the squeamish, shy girl she had been the year before. It would not have bothered her if he had called her to stand up front. She was poised, more confident, and just glad to be back at home and with her friends and family. Stephanie found herself back in the normal routine of things, and it felt good.

Monday came, and it was to be Stephanie's first day back at work with her parents. She rode in to the office with her father. There were plans for her to handle more of the administrative tasks and to assist with site inspections. As she walked in the front door that led to the reception area, Alan was making a pot of coffee near a sink and countertop recently added, and Julie the receptionist was putting on her hands free telephone headset for the day. They heard the front door swing open and looked up.

Alan had a surprised look on his face. "Well, would you look at what just walked in," he said.

"Hi, Stephanie," Julie said.

"Hi, everybody," she replied.

Alan sat the package of coffee granules on the small countertop and rushed over to see her. "Let me take a look at you," he said.

Stephanie said, "How are you?"

Alan wrapped his arms around Stephanie and gave her a hug. Immediately, she noticed something different about him. He seemed thinner than she had remembered. *Too thin*... she thought. Still, it was good to see him.

"Welcome back!" Alan said.

"It's good to be back," she replied.

Alan joked, "Now that I gave you a hug... I don't have to give your father a hug."

Paul smiled. "Hey, we didn't see you at church yesterday. Was everything all right?"

Alan was quick with an excuse. "Oh, I had to take care of some things at the other house."

Stephanie felt Alan was hiding something about his health. However, she did not want to be judgmental and quickly dismissed Alan's peculiar behavior.

Alan asked her how school had been and then told her of his recent change, asking Jesus into his heart.

Stephanie was happy for Alan.

Moments later, Paul ushered Stephanie to his office to go over plans for the day.

It was about two hours into the morning when Russell showed up for work. Stephanie was in her father's office reviewing current building codes when she heard him talking to someone down the hall. She got up out of her chair and stood at the doorway to her father's office. As she looked down the hallway, she saw Russell come into view. He turned and caught a glance of Stephanie peeking out from the office. Suddenly, Russell cut his conversation short at the front desk. He seemed more interested in saying "hello" to Stephanie.

"Well, hey!" he shouted. "Good to see you!"

Stephanie smiled as he walked down the hall. This had been something she had been waiting for. Seeing Russell again was exciting to her. She had wondered how he would look and was pleased to see that he had been taking care of himself. "How *are* you?" she asked him.

"Good," he said.

She walked part way down the hall to meet him half way. There was a smile on her face.

"How was school?" Russell asked.

"Good," she said. "It has its good points and bad."

"Well, it's good to see you," he said.

"It's good to see *you,*" she replied.

Russell could see that she was not the same little girl she was when she left, and in his eyes, it was as if she came back suddenly all grown up. She *was* all grown up.

"Well, maybe we'll have a chance to work together," he said.

"I'm sure we will."

The next day was encouraging for Stephanie as she had hoped to spend more time with Russell. She was working at her father's desk when Russell arrived to work at his usual time. She heard him walking down the hallway as he neared the room. She looked up at the same time he looked in. "Good morning," he said.

She looked small sitting at her father's large desk. "Good morning," she replied.

"How's it going in here?" he asked.

"Good," she said.

Russell walked in the room and looked around. She sat in anticipation of what he would say next.

"I was just wondering if you're going to be working late today," he said.

"Probably not," she said. Suddenly, she could feel the excitement of where his questions were heading. She was sure he was about to ask her out on a date. "I can check with my dad," she said. "He's my ride home."

Immediately, she could feel the heat rushing up the back of her neck.

"Okay," he said nonchalantly.

She looked at him, wondering what he was going to say next. She had already made up her mind, that if he wanted to take her out to supper, then her answer would be "yes."

He stood quiet for a second. "Well," he said, "I was just wondering if you're not going to be in here too late, then it might give me a chance to finish up on that wall shelf I've been meaning to finish up."

Stephanie looked over to the corner where Russell was pointing. She felt a sudden disappointment. She was not interested in any wall shelf, but apparently, he was. It made her mad. "I'll ask my dad how late he wants me here, and let you know," she said.

Russell nodded his head. "That would be great," he said, and then walked out.

Stephanie sat dumbfounded by Russell's sudden cold personality. In her mind, this was not the same Russell. She was almost sure he was about to ask her out on a date, and the conversation ended up being about a wall shelf he had made. She sat in her father's chair feeling confused and suddenly doubted what she had thought was a mutual feeling between her and Russell. It left her feeling empty.

Then Russell reappeared with a smile. "By the way," he said,

"If you're not busy for lunch, I was wondering if you might like to go out and get a bite with me."

Stephanie shook her head, and then smiled at Russell. She looked up as if she wanted to throw her father's electric stapler at him. "No," she said. "I'm afraid I need to design a new wall shelf."

Russell laughed. "Good one," he said. "Does that mean yes?"

Stephanie looked him in the eye and said, "I would love to have lunch with you."

Russell was glad. "I'll see you then."

"See you then," she replied.

Weeks passed. On some days, Stephanie would see Russell as many as three or four times regarding business needs. Occasionally, she would go out and have lunch with him, but not everyday. She was glad to be home with her family, and the few opportunities she had to visit with Russell. She invited him to attend church with her, but he declined. She was nineteen years old now. He was twenty-seven. She wondered what the future would bring as the summer drew near. She hesitated becoming serious with Russell because she would be returning to college in the fall. She was afraid to let a steady relationship get in the way of her college education. She believed God's plan for her was to finish school... then, settle down with marriage only *after* becoming a business entrepreneur. There were many things for her to consider, and often she prayed.

There was one day in July when Stephanie needed to deliver revised blueprints to a building site where Russell had been working. She was happy to go there because it meant she would get to see Russell on the job. To her knowledge, he had no idea she would be the one to deliver the blueprints. She drove one of the company cars to get there, and as she approached the construction site, she saw Russell's truck parked next to several other vehicles belonging to the other crewmembers. She parked behind Russell's truck, hoping to surprise him. As she walked past Russell's truck, she glanced in. There was a bouquet of flowers sitting in the front seat. At first, she did not think much of it. However, as she approached the building to find Russell... she found him all right. He was on the ground floor talking with a woman.

She did not think much about the flowers or Russell talking to a woman, at first. However, suddenly, she started to wonder. She stood out in the yard as the sun was shining down, which made it more difficult for him to see her. Stephanie did not want to be rude in interrupting his conversation with the woman. She appeared to be a professional woman... possibly someone from the bank, but Stephanie was unsure. There were workers up overhead in the two-story structure as they hammered away and sounds of metal clanking against steal pipes.

Fifteen minutes went by, and Stephanie did her best not to be rude and interrupt. She walked around the building and watched as crewmembers steadied sheetrock to install in the upper rooms. One of the them recognized her and said "hi." The impression they had was that she was there to inspect the building, so they did not pay much attention to her presence.

With time passing, Stephanie began to get more concerned about the woman Russell was talking to, and if the flowers in his truck meant anything. Instinctively, she began to feel jealous. It was wrong , and she knew the Lord would be displeased with her for feeling the way she was, but she could not help it. She began to think the worst that Russell was romantically involved with the woman he was talking with, and that *she* must have been the one who gave him the flowers. It bothered her. She stood on the side of the building where there were no windows, and no one could see her. Her eyes began to water as the sun shined brightly upon where she stood. There was dirt beneath her feet that dried as a dusty white powder. Twenty minutes into her wait, finally she saw the woman emerge from the building. She was wearing a blue dress, and looked like someone from a bank or other profession. Stephanie had the gumption to approach the woman and question her business with Russell, but she was too hurt inside to leave the mound of dirt on which she had been standing.

Inside, Russell resumed his inspection of the plumbing and electrical wiring. He yelled up to one of the workers, asking for a hand in moving some of the building materials that were in his way. A man named Charlie came down. Ironically, Charlie was the one who recognized Stephanie at the building site a short while ago. He asked Russell if the inspection went okay.

Russell replied, "What inspection?"

Charlie said, "The inspection. Isn't that why Paul's daughter was here?"

Russell looked out the large open spaces on the front of the building that would eventually house windows. Then, he looked back at Charlie. "Stephanie was here?" he asked.

"Yeah, she was walking around," he said. "I assumed you knew she was here."

Russell was concerned. He walked outside and looked around the front. Then, he stood back and looked up to the second story of the building. Just as he was about to yell up at the other crewmembers, he saw Stephanie standing alone on the side of the building. He ran over toward her wondering why she was standing outside alone.

"Stephanie," he called. "What are you doing?"

She stood facing the gray concrete wall as the afternoon sun beat down on her long brown hair. She had the blueprints rolled up in her hands. She did not turn around to look at him.

Russell could see something was wrong. "Are you okay?" he asked.

She turned her head enough to hand him the blueprints without making eye contact. "I brought you the blueprints," she said.

Russell stepped closer to her. "Why are you upset?" he asked. "What happened?"

"Nothing," she said. Then she started walking back to the car.

Russell stood looking confused. "Is it anything I said?" he asked.

"No," she replied.

Russell watched her walk toward the parking lot. He did not know what to think.

Just as he was about to run to her, she turned and said, "By the way, I like your flowers."

Russell felt like an idiot. Suddenly, he made the connection. "No!" He ran to Stephanie. "No, no, no," he said. "It's not what you think!"

Stephanie stood standing next to his truck. "It's okay," she said. "You and I are just friends. I shouldn't let it bother me if other women give you flowers."

Russell ran to her in an utter frenzy to find the words. He fell upon his knees, and looked up at her. "No, Stephanie. I'm afraid you've come to the wrong conclusion."

She looked at him. "Did I?" she asked.

Russell smiled. "Yes," he said.

There was silence. Stephanie looked up at the building and noticed there were several workers looking down, watching the free show unfolding in the parking lot. She knew they respected Russell greatly, and that he would not be on his hands and knees unless it was for something important. She stood, waiting for him to finish saying what he had to say.

"That woman you saw was Doctor Lambert," he said. "She's the dentist who'll be moving her practice here when it's done."

Stephanie looked at Russell as he remained on his knees.

"Is it customary for clients to give you flowers?" she asked.

Russell started laughing. Stephanie was not amused. "No," he said. "It is not customary for clients to give me flowers, but these flowers are special."

"I need to get going," Stephanie said.

"Wait," Russell said.

Stephanie was getting impatient. From where she was standing, she could see the flowers in the front seat of his truck.

Russell stood up. "Would you at least take a moment to look at the flowers I got? They are real pretty."

"I'm all set," Stephanie said as she looked at her watch.

Russell reached for the door handle on his truck as she stood next to him. She really did not care to see his flowers. She stood out of the way. He opened the truck door. "I just want to show you how pretty these are," he said.

Stephanie looked at him like he was crazy expecting her to admire the flowers from another woman. Then he handed the flowers to her. "I want you to have these," he said.

She looked at the flowers, which included an array of a dozen red roses and baby's breath. Attached was a heart-shaped card that read…

To Stephanie
Love, Russell

Stephanie was lost for words. She felt terrible. She looked at Russell as he stood holding the bouquet of flowers he bought for her. His arms extended out waiting for her to accept the gift. Her eyes started to water. "I'm sorry," she said.

"It's okay."

She gave him a big hug.

Russell smiled. "I would have thought the same thing if I were in your shoes," he said.

"I am so sorry for accusing you of doing wrong," she said.

Russell assured her it was okay.

"Thank you for getting me flowers," she said, still with a tone of apology in her voice.

In the coming weeks, there were other trips to building sites and times when Stephanie would find herself working next to Russell. Their friendship strengthened, and often they would look back and reflect upon that bitter day with the flowers. Slowly, their friendship blossomed into something that gave them both the confidence that they would remain friends for a long time. How long would that last? Neither dared guess. What they knew was that they enjoyed each other's company and looked forward to staying in touch. There were occasional times when Stephanie felt she was losing control of her life. It was clear to her that Russell did not know the Lord, and she felt that she was falling in love with him. She prayed for Russell that he would be saved. What mattered to her most was that she would do what was right according to God, and she pondered whether Russell was part of His plan for her. She wanted to believe that it was.

Alan

Fall came and Stephanie soon found herself back at the University of Wisconsin at Madison. It was a muggy night, which somehow reminded her of the time Alan came to her parents' house to give her a gift. That was more than a year ago. Stephanie reminisced of the summer that had passed. It was a good time. She learned new skills in her trade, and enjoyed getting to know Russell on a more personal level. Alan's health also concerned her. Nobody ever talked about it, but it seemed to her that Alan was not looking well. On the day she left, he was feeling ill. She also noticed that he was not working as many hours at the business. Perhaps this was because Alan was getting near retirement. She wondered about him.

It was a Tuesday night in November, when the phone in her dormitory rang. Stephanie answered the phone and quickly assumed the call was for her roommate who was out with friends. The caller was her mother. This was unusual for a Tuesday night.

"Hi," her mother said.

Immediately, Stephanie knew something was wrong.

"Hi," Stephanie said. "What's up?"

There was a pause in her mother's voice. "It's Alan," she said. "He didn't want anybody to know this, but he's in the advanced stages of lung cancer."

Suddenly, it made sense to Stephanie. The times she noticed his shortness of breath, and his loss of weight… now she knew. She was somewhat shocked by the news. "How can this be?" she asked. "He's never even been a smoker."

"They think maybe he got it from his years of exposure to asbestos when he was younger," Melva replied.

Stephanie felt as if a huge bubble was in her throat, and it was about to pop. Alan had been more than just a family friend to her, he was like the uncle she never had.

There was a pause in the conversation.

"Do you want to talk to your father?" her mother asked.

"Yes," she said.

As her dad picked up the phone, Stephanie was looking at her calendar. "Hi, sweetie," he said. This was the last thing she wanted to hear her father say. He *only* called her "sweetie" when there was something very serious at hand.

"Hi, Dad," she replied.

"How's it going out there?"

"Good."

"How are your studies?" he asked.

"Good."

There was a moment of silence. "Is he going to be all right?" Stephanie asked.

"I wish I could say. He's going in for surgery tomorrow."

"I'll pray for him," Stephanie said.

Her father said, "If it's as bad as the doctors think it is, they won't be able to do much for him."

"Well... tell him I'll see him next week when I come home for Thanksgiving."

There was a pause in her father's voice. "Well, that's what we're calling about," he said.

"I don't understand."

Her father continued, "There's a chance he might not be with us Thanksgiving."

Stephanie did not know what to say. She felt overcome by grief, and tears came to her eyes. "That's not right," she said.

"The Lord's calling him home," her father said.

Paul was never one who liked to spend too much time on the phone, particularly when it involved emotional subjects. He said, "I'm going to hand the phone to your mother now."

"Okay," she said.

Melva got on the phone. "Hello?"

Stephanie was at a loss for words thinking about Russell. She knew Alan was the only family Russell had. He had grown up as an only child and lost his mother at a very young age. She knew she needed to pray for Russell more than ever.

"We're wondering if you would like to come home sooner," her mother said.

Without hesitation, Stephanie said, "Yes."

"We'll make your travel arrangements."

After Stephanie got off the phone with her mother, she began to cry. The thought of losing a close friend and family member deeply saddened her as could be expected. Then, all at once, she remembered that Alan had accepted Jesus Christ as his personal Lord and Savoir, and this gave her a bittersweet reason to rejoice. She prayed for him, and then she prayed for Russell.

It was the Monday before Thanksgiving when Stephanie boarded a plane at Dane County Regional Airfield in Madison. The earliest flight she could get was late in the afternoon. Her wait at the airport seemed to take forever, and then changing planes in Chicago brought more delays. It was nightfall when she finally landed in South Portland, Maine. Her parents were at the airport eagerly waiting to see her. It was both a joyful and sad time because they all knew the reason she had returned home early.

The ride home was somber as Stephanie sat in the back seat of the car reminiscing of Alan, and the way she would remember him forever. He meant so much to her. Her parents sat in the front of the car and were equally quiet. It was difficult for her to know what was going through their minds. She watched as her father repeatedly changed his position in his seat from leaning forward over the steering wheel to sitting back in his seat. It appeared he was tired, and he struggled to stay awake.

Her mother did not move much at all. The latest word was that doctors had operated on Alan and discovered what they feared the most. The cancer spread throughout his lungs and was inoperable. Before Alan had gone into surgery, he told Edna and his son that he did not want to be on life-support if there was no chance of him making a full recovery. Sadly, they were there to see his wishes granted. Both Russell and Edna remained by his father's side throughout the ordeal.

As the highway miles stretched into darkness, the minutes turned into hours. Midnight came before they finally drove into their driveway in Belgrade Lakes. Stephanie had hoped they could stop at the hospital in Augusta before going straight home, but her father was insistent on going home for the night.

The house was dark and cold when they walked in. Stephanie reached into her carry on bag for the University of Wisconsin sweater she brought home from college. She looked around the room as her father turned on the lights. Things were exactly as she remembered them from a couple of months ago, yet felt out of place with Alan being ill. She sat in the rocking chair and watched her father reach for the wood stove and stoke the fire. She could see that not much remained of the burning coals since no one had been home all day. Her mother came into the room and picked up the cordless phone that sat on a nearby stand. She wondered whom her mother might be calling at that late hour. Then, she soon realized it was the nurse's station at the hospital. "Hello," her mother said. "This is Melva Gallagher…"

Stephanie listened to her mother's conversation, hoping to hear positive news. What she gathered was that Alan was still alive and that they expected he probably *would* make it through the night. However, he had not regained consciousness since his surgery.

It was about 1:00 a.m. when Melva got off the phone. She shared the latest update with Paul and Stephanie, and then suggested they all try to get some sleep.

"Will I be able to talk to him?" Stephanie asked.

"Probably not," her father replied. "But, we'll go to see him in the morning."

Stephanie was not ready to go to bed… at least, not in her room. There was something about the night that made her feel the need to stay vigilant. She moved over to the couch to lie down. There was an afghan draped over the back of the couch that her grandmother had made years ago. She pulled it down and tossed it over her. The heat from the woodstove warmed the room. She closed her eyes and silently prayed.

Paul and Melva turned the lights down low and then quietly left the room.

Stephanie awoke on the couch as the sunshine pierced through the curtains that hung over the windows. The room was chilled, and her father came in from outside with an arm full of firewood. Her mother was in the kitchen making coffee. Suddenly, she remembered why she had fallen asleep on the couch. They would be leaving soon to go see Alan.

Stephanie got up off the couch and kept the afghan wrapped around her for warmth. She rubbed her eyes, and her stomach ached at the thought of seeing Alan in a hospital bed. She also wondered if Russell had been able to find any comfort through any of this.

Her father looked up to say "good morning" as he loaded the woodstove with firewood. "How are you doing?" he asked.

"Fine," she said.

Melva heard the two talking and came in to sit down. She had a cup of coffee in her hands. "There is fresh coffee out there," she said, pointing to the kitchen.

Stephanie was sad to know that a good friend was dying, yet at the same time, she counted her blessings to know that both of her parents were with her. It gave her an appreciation to cherish every moment with them she could.

Melva reached for the phone and called the hospital to see how Alan was doing. She was glad to hear that he had survived the night and was coherent. Russell and Edna remained by his side. For Paul, Melva, and Stephanie, this meant they had a chance to see their friend again. They wasted no time in getting ready to drive into town.

The ride to Maine General Hospital was grim because they all knew that with each passing moment, it could be Alan's last. They had hoped to talk with him; however, it was uncertain that he would have the strength or even know who they were. As they arrived at the hospital and walked down the corridor, Melva, Paul, and Stephanie were surprised to find Russell sitting alone in the waiting room. It appeared he was watching television with his head held low and arms supporting his chin. They stood in the hallway and peeked in the room through the glass as he sat unaware of their presence. His eyes were beet red, and it looked as if he had not slept in days. Stephanie felt a mix of emotions as she saw the man who had once appeared to be so confident suddenly broken down and empty. She wanted to run in and give him a hug, but she was hesitant of how he might respond. He sat quietly, looking lonely and confused.

Melva reached for the door that led to the waiting room, and she slowly opened it. Russell looked up as he heard the door hinges squeak. Paul was the first to enter the room. Stephanie followed her father into the room as her mother held the door open. They approached Russell as he sat filled with sorrow.

Melva asked, "Is there anything we can get you?"

He looked up at her. "Dad's sleeping," he said.

Paul put his hands on Russell's shoulders, offering comfort. "Has he been awake much this morning?" he asked.

"Off and on," Russell said.

Melva sat next to Russell and put her left arm across his back.

Stephanie watched Russell as he sat unyielding with his hands between his knees and struggled to hide the tears that rolled down his face. He tried acting as if everything was all right, but she knew that it was not. He seemed distant to her and nothing like the self-confident man he had been before. He sat quietly, preoccupied by the television that played in the corner of the room. The volume was down low, and it was obvious that he was not watching it. However, it provided him with an escape to focus his eyes upon rather than stare people in the eye and show what he was feeling inside. Alan was terminally ill, and doctors were certain that his passing would soon come.

Russell stood up in a restless stance. They could see his father's illness had obviously taken a toll on him. It was clear Russell had not eaten a decent meal or slept in days. Melva asked, "Can I get you anything?"

"No, I'm all right," Russell said. Then, he sat back down in the chair and covered his eyes and rubbed his face. He turned his head to the side and started to weep quietly.

Paul said, "We're here for ya', buddy."

Stephanie felt badly for Russell, and she wished she could take away some of his grief. She prayed for Russell silently in her mind as her parents tried to console him. She knew Russell was not a praying man, so she kept her prayer silent.

Paul said, "We'd like to go in and see him, if that's all right."

Russell looked up at the clock on the wall as if he had a schedule to maintain. "I should go back in there myself," he said.

There was a pause in the room.

"Is it all right if we all go down together?" Paul asked.

Russell looked at Paul as his rose-red cheeks covered with tears. "Dad wouldn't want it any other way," he said.

"Lead us," Paul said.

Russell stood up, and Paul and Melva did the same. He turned to Melva as a child in need of a mother's love. She reciprocated his gesture by putting her arms around him and gave him a hug of love and friendship. Melva understood his grief because she had lost her parents in similar circumstances. Stephanie stood just a few feet away feeling helpless, wanting to do something more for Russell. She leaned in and put her arms around her mother and Russell as a big group hug. Paul did the same. Then, the four walked out of the waiting room and down the hall.

Alan's hospital room was busy as the nurse and Edna stood outside the doorway talking. Pastor James was in the room sitting next to Alan, holding his hand and praying. Edna was happy to see Paul, Melva, and Stephanie walking down the hall. Russell led the way.

"Hey," Edna said, and she left the nurse to greet Paul, Melva, and Stephanie. She gave them all a hug…including Russell. “He’s just up,” she said.

Paul asked, “Is it okay if we go in?”

Stephanie looked into the room from the hallway. Paul and Melva did the same. Pastor James looked over toward the doorway and saw everyone standing there. “Come in, come in,” he said.

Alan was awake, and his eyes lit up when he saw who was standing in the doorway. He delighted to see them. Paul was the first to come into the room. Pastor James stood up from his chair so the others could be close to Alan.

“Hey there, old buddy,” Paul said. “How are you?”

Alan smiled as if trying to be funny. He was obviously weak, and his words were slow, yet, he jokingly asked Paul, “How do you think I am?”

Paul said, “You were always one for jokes.” He looked at Alan and touched his arm. There was an intravenous tube taped across his wrist for morphine drip. “You’re my best friend,” Paul said, and then there was a pause in his words. Paul was becoming emotional to see his long-time best friend in such a weakened, terminal condition. He did his best to stay strong. “You’ve always been my best friend,” he said.

Alan replied, “You too.”

Stephanie and Melva stood from the other side of Alan’s bed. Alan held his hand up to touch them. They both held his hand. There was slowness in the way he moved his arms, yet his grip was strong as he squeezed Stephanie’s hand. He reached out to give her a hug. She leaned in closely to give him a hug. Melva did the same.

Russell stood next to Paul and was glad to see his father awake. “Hi, Dad,” he said. Alan smiled to see his son. This was the happiest time Alan had known since he had arrived at the hospital. To have everyone together was all he could ask for, and for that moment, he was happy inside. Russell placed his right hand on his father's leg, and they all took turns talking with Alan… sharing stories and laughing when they could. Alan's doctor came in the room only briefly and then left to leave the family alone together. They all knew what was to come but did their best to focus on the good times that they had together.

Alan did not want to let go of Stephanie's hand. At one point, he pulled her close to him and whispered something in her ear. She shook her head "yes" and then stood back to look at Russell. None of the others in the room knew what he said to her that day, but they had their suspicions.

Russell leaned in close to his father. "Can I get you some ice water?" he asked.

Alan said, "No, Edna's got me all fixed up," and then he pointed to his tray.

The tray was empty. Edna looked at Russell because they both knew it had been hours since Alan had anything to eat or drink. His memory was slipping, and it appeared he was getting very sleepy as his eyes began to droop heavily.

Stephanie stood alongside Alan and whispered to him. "You have always been an inspiration to me," she said. "Thank you."

Alan squeezed Stephanie's hand. It was becoming difficult for the others in the room to understand what he was saying as his words slowly became slurred. However, she heard every word when he said, "You have always been the apple of my eye…. You will do well."

Pastor James stood closely nearby with his Bible in hand and began reciting scripture. Russell seemed less interested in hearing the Word of God and more interested in spending every moment with his father. However, out of respect for his father, he stayed in the room while Pastor James recited scripture from

Psalm 23. He spoke with conviction, and for a brief moment, it appeared Russell took in what Pastor James had to say.

> The Lord is my Shepard, I shall not want. He maketh me to lie down in green pastures: He leadeth me beside the still waters. He restoreth my soul: he leadeth me in the paths of righteousness for his name's sake. Yea, though I walk through the valley of the shadow of death, I will fear no evil: for thou art with me… thy rod and thy staff, they comfort me. Thou preparest a table before me in the presence of mine enemies: thou anointest my head with oil; my cup runneth over. Surely goodness and mercy shall follow me all the days of my life: and I will dwell in the house of the LORD for ever. (Psalm 23:1–6)

Stephanie was somewhat at peace to know she had the opportunity to see Alan one last time. Alan died later that morning as Russell, Edna, Paul, Melva, and Stephanie looked on. They all said their goodbyes and then huddled around Alan as he passed into the presence of the Lord.

Russell felt uncomfortable when Paul said that they should rejoice in the Lord. It upset him, and he walked out of the room. Stephanie looked at her father as if asking him what she should do. "It's okay," he said.

Stephanie left the room to find Russell. She watched from down the hallway as he went back into the waiting room. It left her wondering how she could help him, if at all. She walked down the hall toward the waiting room, curious if he was okay. He was sitting alone with his eyes covered by his hands, and crying. Afraid to upset him further, she slowly turned and walked away.

Alan's funeral was on the Saturday after Thanksgiving. No one had seen or heard from Russell since his father's death. Edna and Melva coordinated all the arrangements.

Many people attended Alan's funeral, which took place at the small country church. He did not have much family, but his friends were enough to make it standing room only. Pastor James conducted the service, which lasted about an hour, and Paul gave a wonderful eulogy. Russell sat in the front row dressed in a fine-tailored black suit, and Stephanie sat in an adjoining pew.

Stephanie felt bad for Russell because she knew that he lost the only man in his life who meant everything to him. As she listened to the words of Pastor James, she appreciated the way he spoke of salvation and of Alan's commitment to the Lord that came late in his life. She wondered if anything Pastor James said made sense to Russell. For the most part, Russell just sat solemnly staring at the floor. He was not himself, and it bothered her. She wanted to reach out and somehow tell Russell that everything was going to be okay. Losing a loved one was never easy, but she felt it must be worse when someone does not know God. She wondered if Russell believed in God at all.

After the funeral, everyone seemed to approach Russell and offer condolences. Russell, overwhelmed with emotion, struggled to deal with the loss of his father. Stephanie watched as Russell stood alone. Then Edna approached Russell. It was obvious that Edna cared deeply for Alan. She reached out to Russell with empathy.

"Your father was a good man," Edna said to Russell.

Edna and Melva organized the proceedings that followed the service. There were sandwiches and refreshments set up in the church annex where people celebrated Alan's life. In the center of the room was an easel that displayed a picture of Alan and the quote, "In Loving Memory of Alan Holland."

Russell spent a great deal of his time at the event isolated from everybody. Nothing anybody could say or do seemed to help him feel any better. Then, it occurred to Stephanie what was bothering Russell so much. She watched as he left the room.

Russell walked outside in the churchyard where brown grass covered the partially frozen ground. He stood alone near the corner of the church parking lot, as it remained filled with vehicles belonging to friends that were there to attend his father's wake. The larger vehicles served as a backdrop to him where he could hide from the reality of his father's passing. Stephanie followed him outside for a chance to talk with him alone.

The temperatures were cold that day, and windy conditions prevailed. Russell was walking along a tree line in the far corner of the churchyard when Stephanie approached him. "Hey you," she said. "It's cold out here."

Russell did not pay much attention to her.

"Aren't you cold?" she asked.

"Yeah, it's cold," he said.

"Why don't you come in and stay warm?"

Russell seemed angry. "I can't be in there," he said. "I needed to get out."

Stephanie tried to offer him comfort by saying, "People in there care about you. We all know what you are going through."

"No, you don't," he said in a quick sarcastic response.

Stephanie paused, surprised by his temper. It upset her that he seemed to be directing his anger toward her. She started to take it personally. "You're wrong," she said. "I *do* understand what you are going through."

Russell stood clenching his fingers in a way that displayed his frustration. She watched as his jaw moved about inwardly on the side of his face as he ground his teeth. He seemed to be harboring a great deal of resentment. He yelled at Stephanie, "It feels like a circus in there," he said. "I lost my father, and people seem happy. You want me to be happy… I can't… I'm sorry. I just don't buy into this church stuff, and I don't feel like celebrating right now."

Stephanie was without words. She had never seen Russell so upset about anything before. He turned his back on her, and she began to regret going outside to talk with him. She looked up into the cloud covered blue sky and began to feel empty. She prayed, *Heavenly Father, be with Russell. Help him to know the way, Lord… in Jesus' name. Amen*

Stephanie opened her eyes and saw Russell standing in the same place. He stood quietly as if he was waiting for her to leave. "I love you," she said softly.

Russell did not respond. Stephanie did not expect him to say anything. She turned around and went back inside the church annex without looking back.

Russell Mourns

About a week had passed since Alan's funeral, and Russell returned to the little house that his father had bought. It was Russell's house now, and he liked staying there because it reminded him of his father.

The business, Paul's of New England, was without half of its ownership. With Alan gone, that meant Russell would become the heir to his father's estate. Russell was aware of this, however he did not give it much thought. He spent most of his days and nights at the small house reminiscing of the times he enjoyed with his father. Edna would occasionally check up on him to make sure he was doing all right. For the most part, Russell preferred to be alone.

It happened one day when a man dressed in a suit came to the door. Russell was not interested in answering it, but he knew the man would probably keep coming back, so he opened the door. An attorney from downtown, who represented his father, wanted to discuss his father's will. The man's name was Mr. Reed. Russell let him in, and the two sat down to talk.

Mr. Reed said, "I am very sorry about your father's passing."

"Thank you," Russell said.

"I am here to discuss your father's will which he had asked me to do before he died."

Mr. Reed opened a briefcase and began taking out documents and paperwork. There was a letter that his father had written giving instructions to the handling of his estate. Russell immediately recognized his father's signature at the bottom of the letter.

"Sir," Mr. Reed said, "your father has left you with a very large estate."

Russell looked at Mr. Reed and showed no emotion. He thought it was interesting that Mr. Reed called him "sir." He looked at Mr. Reed and said, "Okay."

"Your father asked me to review these documents with you at a time that was convenient for you. Is now a good time?"

Russell scratched his head. "Sure."

The man proceeded to go over financial records of his father's earnings at Paul's of New England and investments and stocks that his father owned. "These are yours now," Mr. Reed said.

Russell said, "Okay."

Mr. Reed sat there at the table surprised by Russell's lack of interest. He assumed that it was probably too soon after his father's death to be discussing court documents. "Would there be a better time we can go over this in greater detail?" he asked.

"No, that's okay," Russell said. "Now is fine."

Mr. Reed said, "I can continue to handle this estate for you if you would like me to. All you need to do is sign a couple of documents, and basically everything will be taken care of for you. I will make sure you have what you need, when you need it."

Russell looked at the paperwork the man had brought. Some of the financial records he saw were staggering. Russell had no idea how much money his father had invested.

Mr. Reed said, "Basically, you don't need to work for a living anymore."

Russell sat back in his chair and thought about it. He soon realized Mr. Reed was not only there because of his father's request, but also there on behalf of the lawyers that represented his father. They did not want to lose the business of managing such a large estate.

For some strange reason, Mr. Reed felt the need to keep "selling" his services to Russell. He looked around the room of the small house and was intrigued that a man worth so much money would spend so much time in a house that was unfinished and lacked modern conveniences. The drapes that hung from the windows were in disarray, and the furniture was old. Mr. Reed could not believe how bad off the floors were or the fact that the ceiling showed water stains from a small leak in the roof. He said to Russell, "You could take your money and get out of this rat hole."

Russell's face changed color in a rage of temperate fury. "I think you should leave now," he said angrily.

Mr. Reed asked, "Did I say something offensive?"

"Yeah, you did," Russell replied.

"I'm sorry," he said quickly, in an attempt to regain Russell's trust.

Russell stood up from the chair where he was sitting and walked over to the door. Mr. Reed quickly realized he offended Russell. "My deepest apologies," he said. "Please, forgive me."

It was too late. Russell stood at the doorway with his hand on the door handle and opened the door.

Mr. Reed stood up from the chair, regretting the words that came out of his mouth. "I'm sorry, sir."

Russell said, "You'll be hearing from me... when I'm ready to take my business elsewhere."

Mr. Reed gathered his paperwork and put everything back in his briefcase. "I am deeply sorry," he said.

Russell stood with the door open as the cold air from outside filled the house. Mr. Reed walked past Russell and down the tiny front steps. He turned to make one last plea with Russell, but the door closed before he had the chance.

It was the second week in December when Stephanie decided to go out and find Russell. She had continued to help her parents out at the business and postpone her return to college. However, her time was running out. She knew she *needed* to get back in school to maintain her grades in Madison; however, Christmas vacation was right around the corner, and that meant she would be returning to Maine in just a matter of weeks. There was so much going on; she did not feel right about going back to school without saying goodbye to Russell. She would not feel right leaving a friend hanging in the limbs. Russell was still very special to her, and she knew it was only right to reach out to him. She had prayed about it often and felt in her heart that she was doing the right thing.

It was the night before her trip back to Wisconsin when she decided to pay Russell a visit. She had heard from Edna at church that Russell was staying at the small house alone. She wanted to make sure he was going to be okay. She loved him as she loved all children of God. She did not know if God's plans for her included Russell, but she knew it was only right to witness to him if there was an opportunity.

Stephanie drove her mother's car after dark to find the small house Edna described. It was a Saturday evening after supper. Stephanie did not have much of an appetite and told her parents what she wanted to do. They trusted her judgment.

As she drove out that night, she began to prepare herself for

Russell's rejection. At the very least, she had hoped she would find Russell home and that perhaps he would be willing to come to the door. The drive over was unnerving due to the road conditions, as it had begun to snow.

When Stephanie arrived, she was relieved to see there really *was* a house at the end of the long dirt road that led into the woods. If not for the sign Wilson Pond Road, she would have not dared to venture down the desolate looking road. As she pulled into the yard, the lights were on and Russell's pick-up truck was in the yard. She drove in and parked behind his truck. She wanted to call, but Russell did not have a phone. She got out of her car and stepped into the darkness of his driveway. The headlights to her mother's Volvo remained on for about five seconds, and then everything went dark.

Through the curtains in the kitchen window, she could see Russell inside sitting on his couch. He stood up to look outside, and she walked slowly hoping he would be glad to see her. Russell opened the front door of the house and struggled to see who was in his yard. "Hello," he said. "Who's there?"

Stephanie was almost afraid to say it was she. Then he heard her small voice come from the darkness.

"Hi," she said.

Russell seemed lost for words.

"I was hoping I could find you here," Stephanie said as she slowly made her way into the dim light that emitted from a lamp inside the house.

"Stephanie?" he asked. "Is that you?" Then, he could see her. She stood still at the bottom of his steps and looked up at him. She wore a red jacket and had dark colored mittens and a hat.

"I apologize for showing up like this," she said. "But, I couldn't go back to college without making sure you are going to be okay."

Russell seemed happy to see her. "Please," he said, "won't you come in?"

She walked up the small steps and into the house.

Russell closed the door and then looked at her. She looked at him. He had not shaved in at least a week. It was a new look for him, and one she had not seen before. He looked around the room and suddenly felt embarrassed that he had not done any cleaning for a while. "If I knew you were coming, I would have straightened up a bit," he said.

Stephanie replied, "That's okay. I'm just glad to see you."

Russell looked at her, as though he had not seen anyone in a year. "You look great," he said. "I can't believe you came out to see me."

"I've been worried," she said. "Everyone's been worried about you."

"I would have turned on an outside light," he said, "but the bulb blew and I haven't felt like replacing it. I think I'll do that right now."

Stephanie smiled. "That's okay," she said. "It is good to see you."

There was softness in Russell's demeanor. It looked as though he let go of the anger that had built up inside of him on the day of his father's funeral. He looked at Stephanie. "It is good to see you," he said.

Stephanie looked around the room. "It's nice here."

Russell said, "Dad and I were going to fix it up, but we never got the chance. He was never one who liked to leave anything unfinished."

"He was a great man," Stephanie said.

"Would you like a tour?" he asked.

"I'd like that," she said.

Russell seemed to be opening up to her. He was cordial and

sincere. *This* was the Russell she had remembered falling head over heals for.

He noticed she was still bundled in her winter jacket, hat, and mittens. "Can I help you with those?" he asked.

"Thanks," she said, and then handed him her coat. He hung it up on a coat rack next to the door. There was a ceramic cookie jar on his countertop in the form of Cookie Monster from Sesame Street. He put her hat on the cookie jar to be funny, and then set her mittens on each side of the cookie jar. It looked like Cookie Monster was ready for a cold night.

"How about a cup of coffee or cocoa?" he asked.

"Cocoa sounds good. Thank You."

As Russell reached for a couple of cups from the cupboard, Stephanie sat down at the little kitchen table.

"I'll be going back to Wisconsin tomorrow," she said. "I didn't want to leave without saying goodbye."

"Thank you for that," Russell said. Then he filled the cups with water and placed them in his microwave. "How about that tour?" he asked.

Stephanie stood up. "I'm ready," she said.

Jokingly, Russell set the timer on his microwave for three minutes and said, "If we start now, this will be finished about the time the tour is over."

Stephanie giggled. "You mean this house is that small, or are we going to be running?" she asked.

"It's small," he said.

As the microwave started, he began to show her around the room.

Stephanie admired the details of the handiwork. "How much of this is original?" she asked.

"All of it," Russell said.

The cupboard doors were hand-made and featured handcrafted decorations from a router. Everything was unfinished, including the pine woodwork trim that bordered the room. To the right, there was a small rustic style living room and couch, and to the left was the kitchen. As they walked downstairs, she began to get a sense of how small the house really was. It was cute though, and she liked what she saw. Below, there was a small living space not much bigger than a one-car garage. Russell was able to show her the backyard terrace since the light was still working.

As he led her back up the stairs, the tour was over. The microwave timer was in its last few seconds.

"See," Russell, said. "What did I tell you?"

She laughed.

Russell snickered, "It's a pretty small place, but I like it. I don't think I'll ever get rid of it."

"I don't blame you," Stephanie said. "It's not about the money. It's about hanging on to something with sentiment."

Everything Stephanie was saying to Russell made sense to him. She sat quietly while he made the hot cocoa. She knew she cared about him deeply, and feelings of longing to have something more than just a friendship were starting to surface.

Russell understood that Stephanie was sincere in visiting him, and it meant a lot to him that she took the time to find him on a cold dark night.

Their visit quickly turned into an hour, and then two. Stephanie looked at her watch and began to worry that her parents might be concerned. "I just want to give them a call," she said, and then got up from her seat to reach for the cell phone that was in her jacket pocket. She turned the phone on and made the call. Her mother answered the phone. Melva was glad to hear from her daughter and told her not to rush home. "Drive safe," was all she said.

Stephanie felt glad to have her mother's reassurance, and then she suddenly thought of how difficult it must be for Russell not having a mother or father to turn to. She thought of the Lord, and how having a *Heavenly Father* is a blessing. She hoped for an opportunity to share the good news of the Lord with Russell, but she was also afraid to bring back a bad memory. She knew high pressure was not the way to convert anyone. It would take time, she thought.

Stephanie was beginning to feel so much more for Russell. She could see the goodness of who he was, and that he really just needed someone to help him along in life. As their conversation continued, she saw all of his good qualities. He did most of the talking, and inside she was just glad to be in his presence.

They both had refills on the cocoa, and then took their conversation over to his small couch where it was more comfortable. It did not matter to her that he had not shaved in a week, or if his socks were dirty… she saw the goodness of his heart and felt very attracted to him. She began to hope that the evening might end with a hug. However, her conscience reminded her that she could also be vulnerable to anything Russell wanted. She knew there had to be limits. How far might a hug go? She wondered. Stephanie was a very affectionate person. She wanted to make sure her intentions were right with God. Then she remembered a portion of scripture concerning affection: *Set your affection on things above, not on things on the earth* (Colossians 3:2). It reminded her of her purpose for visiting with Russell in the first place. She had come to witness to him.

Russell rambled on about the plans he had with his father to renovate the small house. “The plans were to build a bedroom outwards toward the right,” he said. “Then make another one downstairs with a fireplace.”

“It sounds wonderful,” Stephanie said.

“Then upstairs, we were going to put in a big lofty bedroom, with a spiral staircase.”

Russell looked around the room. She could see the enthusiasm in his voice when he talked about the plans his father had with him. It was as if Russell intended to finish where his father left off.

By 10:00 p.m., Stephanie and Russell sat closely on the couch as though they had escaped the barrier that was between them, and they found themselves becoming nervous about being alone together. The room was dark where they sat, and the thought of touching stirred up feelings within both of them that they had never experienced. Russell knew he was beginning to care very deeply for this woman, and although there was an eight-year difference in their ages, he put that aside. Stephanie knew she was attracted to Russell, and she knew he was attracted to her. More and more, their actions became flirtatious.

At one point, Russell's foot accidentally touched hers, and she kicked him back with a light tap. "Keep your foot on your own side of the couch," she said, trying to be funny.

Russell played along. "It *is* my side of the couch," he said. "Your foot attacked me."

Then, Stephanie looked down at her foot and said, "Bad foot!" She scolded it for flirting. They both laughed.

In Russell's mind, he wanted to hold Stephanie tight, and he began to imagine how it would feel to have her in his arms and loving her with all his heart. Falling in love suddenly felt like it would be easy. However, he feared being too forward with her and ruining what seemingly had become a mutual friendship. They continued to talk about anything they could think of. Without thinking, Russell slowly took the cup of cocoa from Stephanie's hands and gently set it on a small nearby lamp stand.

Stephanie dismissed Russell's flirtatious gesture and acted nonchalant to Russell's intention. "I really like the rug you have in here," she said.

Russell smiled. "Me too," he said. "It matches the rest of the house."

"This is really a great house," she said. "And I like the area. It's nice out here. Quiet... I like that."

"Me too," Russell said.

Soon, it was hard for Stephanie to ignore Russell's increased interest in her. She noticed there was softness in his voice, and he was gentle in the way he moved. She found herself attracted to him more than she could recall and felt warm and fuzzy to be near him. The dim lighting of the room and peacefulness of the small house was comforting to her, and in her heart she was content to be where she was. It was difficult to resist wanting more, and she felt his feelings were the same. As he turned away from her to set his cup of cocoa on the stand next to hers, she saw what she thought was a spider on his arm. With an unexpected swat, she attempted to whisk the small spider away. Russell never saw it coming. Before he could set his cup on the stand, his arm jolted causing him to spill cocoa on his pant leg. "Oh!" she yelled. "I am so sorry."

Russell laughed as he turned around, wondering why she hit him.

"It looked like you had something crawling on you," she said.

He remained seated and set the cup on the lamp stand while trying to hold the laughter back. He turned to check his arm for the insect she claimed to see. There was a dark piece of lint on his shirt. "You mean this?" he asked

Stephanie looked closer to see a tiny piece of lint. She felt embarrassed for mistaking the lint for a spider. "I am so sorry," she said.

Jokingly he asked, "Up to your old tricks again?"

She smiled, almost as if to be hiding her face in shame. "I am so sorry. I'll buy you some new pants."

"That won't be necessary. These old pants are fine," he said. Russell was very patient with spilled cocoa. He almost seemed to enjoy the added sympathy she was giving him.

"Are you sure?" she asked.

"Definitely," he said.

"Can I get you something to dry you off with?" she asked.

"No, this is nothing. It will dry. It's just a little cocoa."

She sat in amazement staring at Russell for his patient demeanor. He was not a man consumed by materialism or one who worried about outward appearances so much. She could see that he was someone who was equally glad to be with her as she was with him.

"You know what I want to do?" Russell asked.

She was almost afraid to answer his question. "No," she said. Then trustingly, with almost a slight nervousness she asked, "What is it you want to do?"

Slowly, he gently moved closer toward her. She sat in anticipation wondering what he was going to do. In her mind, she knew what was going to happen next and wondered if she would have the strength to stop him. It was not strength in muscles she needed, but the strength to hold back from doing something she might regret. Still, she enjoyed playing along with Russell's game as their flirtatious banter continued.

Russell asked, "When did you first know you liked me?"

His question took her by surprise. She had assumed that he would try to hold her hand or make a pass at her when he moved closer. Rather, here he was innocently asking her a question. She was almost disappointed, but delighted to answer his question. Without hesitation she said, "It was the day we first met, and we were in my mother's office. After we cleaned up the mess and went to the broom closet, your hand touched mine. That moment I knew you were not the evil person that I first thought you were, and I had the most major crush on you."

Russell smiled. "I will never forget that day. You tried to take me out. Literally," he said jokingly.

Stephanie looked up at him as he sat close to her on the couch. "When was the first time you knew you had feelings for me?" she asked.

"Believe it, or not," he said. "It was the day we were at my father's funeral. With all the people who had been coming up to me offering condolence, you were the *one* person who helped me feel that I still had someone I could turn to. I knew then that you were a true friend, just in the way you looked at me. And I see that today."

Stephanie smiled at Russell as she looked into his eyes. She was smitten with his charm.

Russell added, "And I never told you this, but I want to tell you now. I regretted acting the way I did. I was just not used to having so many people care about me, or in being in a church where people celebrate a person's life. I did not understand it back then, but I do now. And I feel I owe you an apology."

"You don't owe me an apology," she said. "I know it was a hard time for you. We all go through things."

"Thank you for understanding," Russell said.

Stephanie felt a connection with Russell, and it began to warm her from the inside out as she realized it was from him… not the cocoa. She gazed into his eyes, and then surprised herself. "You can put your arm around me, if you want to." She could not believe she said that.

"I'd like that," Russell said, and then he leaned over to touch her.

She sat awkwardly, reaching up to touch his right hand as he put it over her right shoulder. He was a gentle man and careful not to let his hand come in full contact with her right arm. It was almost an awkward moment for both of them, but they felt content to be in each other's company.

There was a chill in the room, and she whispered to Russell, "Hold me."

"All right," he said, and then he pulled her toward him gently.

Stephanie looked into his eyes with his same desires. She imagined what it would be like to marry such a man and to know the kind of love when two people kiss deeply. The thought of this made her want more. Yet, she was careful not to lead him on.

Russell looked at her with the same kind of wants and needs, and they both resisted the temptation. He looked deeply into her eyes, and knew that she cared for him. The room was silent. "So, do you still?" he asked.

Stephanie asked, "Do I still what?"

Russell said, "You know… what you said earlier, that you had the most major crush on me. Do you still feel that way?"

"Yes," she replied without hesitation.

"Oh," he replied.

Stephanie was enjoying Russell's company, but seemed surprised by his lack of aggressiveness. Slowly, she leaned slightly closer to him and hoped he might kiss her. Russell wanted to feel his lips on hers yet held back just to enjoy the warmth of her body next to his. He knew that he was falling in love with Stephanie but wanted everything to be right. He lifted her chin slightly, and then lowered his face to hers until their lips met.

Stephanie smiled. "That was unexpected," she said, trying to act as if it was a surprise.

Russell said, "You are so beautiful."

Stephanie looked at the clock that was hanging on the wall. "I'm sorry I have to leave soon."

"I hope that we'll get to see each other again," he said.

Stephanie looked at him with certainty. "Of course we will," she said. "I need to finish a semester in school and I'll be back. We should try to keep in touch."

"Okay," Russell said.

Time passed, and soon Stephanie and Russell moved from the couch to the door where he offered to walk her out to her car. "I'll be all set," she said. "I just need my coat."

The small kitchen was dark and lit only by the lamp in the living room. "I'll get that for you," Russell said, and he reached for her coat, which hung on a coat rack in the corner of the doorway.

Stephanie saw her mittens sitting on the Cookie Monster cookie jar and picked them up. Before leaving, she turned to Russell to say goodnight. She wondered if he would kiss her again. With her hand on the doorknob and holding the door ajar, she looked back up at Russell.

"Thanks for coming," Russell said.

"You're welcome," she replied. "Thanks for letting me in."

Then Russell leaned down toward her and kissed her on the lips. Stephanie took her mitten-covered hand off the doorknob and reached her arms up over Russell's shoulders. They both knew in their hearts this was the start of something special, that Stephanie and Russell had become more than just friends.

The ride home for Stephanie was filled with instant replays of the entire evening. The memory of how they sat peacefully on the couch with a warm embrace would be something she would keep with her until she could see him again. Although she had not witnessed to Russell as she thought she would, she was pleased with how the evening had gone. She wondered if Russell was the man that God had chosen for her. It would be something she knew she could pray about, and the memory of seeing Russell made it easier for her to go back to Wisconsin. She knew he would be okay.

Paul's Accident

It was just two days after Stephanie returned to college when it had began to snow in Madison. Her schooling was challenging because she had a lot of catching up to do. She believed her education was what God wanted for her; however, her heart was still back in Maine.

Coincidentally, it had also begun to snow in Maine over Belgrade Lakes. Paul and Melva were doing their best to cope with the loss of Alan. The day brought forth light flurries with light accumulation. Temperatures were below freezing.

Paul needed to use this day to visit a building site that was behind schedule. An inspection was overdue, and there was a push to get the job done.

At the construction site, Paul climbed a ladder to look at a second story floor joist. An overcast sky and cold winds prevailed as the early morning sun had barely begun to shine. The weather forecast called for snow, so he knew time would be limited to complete the outside work. Crews were already working inside the structure when he arrived.

As Paul carefully made his way across the second story scaffolding, snow and ice covered the panels that provided footing. There was a pipe laying on one of the boards, and without warning, Paul stepped on the pipe, which caused him to slip. In a desperate attempt to catch his fall, he reached up to one of the cross-member poles, which was iced over from snow that had melted the day before. He fell to the ground and appeared to be hurt badly. Roger, a nearby supervisor, heard the noise and ran to see what had happened. He saw his boss lying on the ground with his back covered with snow.

"Boss!" he yelled.

Paul was lying face down on the ground and moaning.

"Boss, are you all right?" he asked frantically.

Paul did not respond.

Then he could see Paul slowly turn onto his side, as he lay there on the snow-covered ground. The clipboard Paul brought with him to the construction site was on the ground next to him. Roger got on his knees and crouched down to comfort Paul. "I'll get you a doctor," he said.

Paul struggled to speak, but the pain brought tears to his eyes. Roger feared the worst had happened. "You stay right here, Boss, I'll get you some help."

"My leg," Paul said. "It's my leg."

"I'm gonna call 9–1-1. Everything's gonna be all right," Roger said in a desperate attempt to calm his boss.

"Help," he yelled out to get the attention of someone with a cell phone. Roger took his coat off and laid it over Paul to help keep him warm. One of the workers from within the building heard Roger yelling and came to see what had happened. Roger looked up to the man. "Call 9–1-1!" he yelled. "We got a hurt man here."

"I'm on it," the man said as he reached for his cell phone.

Roger stayed with Paul and gently put his arms over Paul to

keep him warm. "Everything's gonna be all right, Boss. We got help on the way."

Paul was starting to catch his breath. It looked as though he was having trouble breathing. Roger knew little about CPR, yet instinctively checked Paul for vital signs. Paul appeared to be okay, except his leg was obviously broken, and it looked like he had the wind knocked out of him.

"I can't breathe," Paul said.

"Everything's gonna be all right," Roger said. "We got an ambulance on the way."

Within minutes, an ambulance had arrived. Paramedics quickly checked Paul's vital signs and talked to him. Paul was able to communicate well as they worked to carefully put him on a stretcher and into the ambulance.

Roger said, "I'll let Melva know to meet us at the hospital."

Stephanie was at college, trying to focus on her studies and the thought of Russell remained on her mind. It was hard to focus on her schoolwork. She felt positive that she had done the right thing in returning to school; however, something still felt out of place. She reminisced of the night she shared hot cocoa with Russell at his house, and it seemed to have a way of keeping her warm on the inside. However, she also longed to go back and feel the warmth of his arms around her again.

That evening in her dorm room, Stephanie felt alone and confused. She wanted to call Russell. As she was trying to study for an upcoming math exam, she realized she was in love with Russell. Every word on the page and every math problem she tried to solve had Russell's name on it. The thought of him weighed heavy on her mind.

Stephanie knew she needed to place the ordeal in God's hands if she was to get ready for her exam.

She slid from her chair and knelt on the floor with her elbows resting on the side of her small bed. "Dear Lord," she prayed. "Please help me. Guide me with every step I take. Help me to do what is right." She did not want to leave Russell out... "Also, be with Russell, Lord. Help him to know your love, and if it is your will for he and I to be together, show us the way. Amen."

Stephanie stood up and was glad she shared her concerns with God. She was confident He would see her through. There was a chill in the room, and she knew it would be about an hour before her roommate returned. This was her chance to study all that she could in the time that remained. Just then, the phone rang. She answered the phone, and assumed it was for her roommate.

"Hello," she said.

There was a silence on the other end of the receiver. Then, she heard a faint "Hi." It was her mother.

Stephanie could tell by the tone of her mother's voice that something was dreadfully wrong. She immediately feared that Russell might have fallen into a depression and done something drastic. "Don't tell me," she said.

"Your father's been in an accident," her mother said.

Stephanie was shocked to hear the news. "How is he?" she asked.

"He's going to be all right," Melva said. "He's got a severely broken leg and several broken ribs."

Stephanie felt guilty about praying for her needs and not the needs of others.

"Your father's going to be in the hospital for a while," she said.

"How long?" she asked.

"They don't know yet," her mother replied.

Stephanie was starting to regret her decision to return to college. She thought she was doing what God wanted of her, but now she was feeling confused. This was not part of God's plan in her mind. This was not supposed to happen.

"I want to come home," Stephanie told her mother.

"What about school?" her mother asked.

"I can make it up," Stephanie said. "I think it would be best if I just come home and be with you and Dad."

There was a moment of silence. "Why don't you come home," her mother suggested.

Stephanie knew she needed to be with her parents, and in the back of her mind, she knew this also meant she would see Russell. Her mind was in a state of confusion as to whether or not she was doing the right thing. She prayed about it briefly while on the phone with her mother, and in an instant she replied, "All right, I'll come home."

Her mother was pleased with Stephanie's decision, and the two had agreed that she would postpone her studies for an indefinite period.

The next day, a one-way flight from Madison, Wisconsin, to South Portland, Maine, was in order.

It was the next day before Paul came to the realization that he was in the hospital. He felt restrained from sitting up in his bed. Melva stood next to him beneath a small television that hung from the wall. Pastor James was present, and Roger the supervisor was there. Paul looked at everyone. "What are you all doing here?" he asked.

"You had an accident," Melva said. "You slipped on some ice."

"I did?" Paul asked. He seemed confused. "What time is it?" he asked.

Roger looked at the clock on the wall. "It's about two o'clock," he said.

Paul was concerned about the building inspection. "We've got to get that inspection done. The deadline is today," he said.

"That was yesterday," Roger said.

Melva tried to calm Paul. "You need your rest," she said.

Roger assured his boss. "We're all set with the inspection," he said. "I called Charlie, and he took care of it."

Paul rubbed his eyes. "Where's my coat?" he asked.

Melva answered, "You're not going anywhere. You've been in a serious accident."

"I feel fine," Paul said. Then he tried sitting up and the pain set it. He looked around and saw an intravenous tube taped to his arm. The pain was starting to get uncomfortable. Melva explained to him what happened.

"You just need to stay relaxed," she said.

Just then, a nurse entered the room. "Is everything okay?" she asked.

"Somebody's ready to go home," she said jokingly.

The nurse looked at Paul as she reached for his chart. "How are we doing, Mr. Gallagher?"

"Been better," he said.

"That was quite a fall you took," she said.

Melva asked, "How long do you think he'll need to stay?"

"I'll go get the doctor," the nurse said then left the room.

Melva was concerned that Paul might try to get up and hurt himself worst. "You broke your leg," she said. "Do you remember the doctors taking x-rays and setting your bones back in place?"

"No," he said. "I don't remember anything. Last thing I knew, I was doing an inspection."

Melva was concerned that Paul may have hit his head harder than the doctors thought. Just then, the doctor came in.

"How are we doing?" the doctor asked with enthusiasm.

"Fine," Paul said. "How long am I going to be here?"

"Well, for a while," he said.

The doctor held Paul's x-rays up to the light and explained his concerns about the broken leg and ribs. "You won't be going home tonight," he said. "This much we know."

"I can't stay here," Paul said. "I've got a business to run."

The doctor looked at him with compassion. "I understand," he said. "But, it's going to be at least six weeks before you're ready to do anything."

Melva could see the look of concern on Paul's face. The doctor left the room.

Melva said, "I called Stephanie, and she'll be coming home later today."

Paul seemed happy to hear the news.

Pastor James talked with Paul and suggested they pray for Stephanie's safe return and for the healing of his body. They prayed together.

Paul was grateful to have people by his side.

A short time later, Roger left after giving his boss assurance that the building crews would continue while he recovered from the accident. There were brief discussions about who would fill in for Paul while he was out of work. No one had an answer. Melva assured him not to worry. "God will provide," she said.

Stephanie Steps In

Almost immediately after arriving back at home, Stephanie was in a "take-charge" kind of mood. She was concerned for her father's health and spent many hours at the hospital with him. Russell was on her mind; however, her father's well-being was her greatest concern.

Stephanie spent the day with her father on his third day in the hospital. She could see that the effects of his fall had taken a toll on his body. He looked tired, and the pain was excruciating. Stephanie prayed for God to relieve her father's pain. Still, she and her mother knew that time would need to pass in order for him to heal.

Melva left the room to get something to drink. Stephanie looked at her father as he expressed concerns about who would run their construction business. All at once, she saw this as an opportunity to help. She said to him, "I can help with the business."

"That would be nice," her father said. "Your mother could use some help in the office, but I still need someone who can run the business."

Stephanie struggled to convince her father. "You don't understand," she said. "I can run the business until you get better."

Paul started to chuckle, "Don't make me laugh… it hurts." He said, "I appreciate what you're offering, but there's a lot to it."

Stephanie assured him. "I can do it," she said.

"What do you know about building codes?" he asked.

"I know a lot," she said. "It's the kind of thing I've been studying for."

Paul smiled. "It's a lot of information to know."

Stephanie said, "If there's something I don't know I can always come to you to find the answer."

"True," her father said.

Melva walked in the room, catching only part of the conversation. Stephanie looked at her mother and said, "Dad's going to let me run the business."

Melva looked at Paul. "You are?" she asked.

Paul was hesitant in giving his answer. He looked at Stephanie. "She could do a good job," he said.

Melva looked at Paul as if the doctors gave him too much painkiller. "I agree she could probably do it. But, are you sure she is ready?"

Stephanie looked at her mother. "I'm ready," she said. "Besides, it's only temporary."

Melva trusted that her daughter had the ability yet was afraid some of the crewmembers would be disrespectful toward her because of her age. She started to ask, "What about… "

Paul interrupted. "She'll be fine," he said.

"Okay," Melva replied and then looked at her daughter. "Do you really want to do this?" she asked.

Stephanie spoke with confidence. "More than you know," she said.

Melva could see Stephanie's conviction. "Well, okay," she said. "Sounds like you've got the job."

Paul rested his head quietly between two pillows. His bed was tilted upward allowing him to sit forward. He looked comfortable, providing he did not move. He was confident that Stephanie had the aptitude to fill in for him while he would be recovering. "She'll do great," he said.

Stephanie smiled with a look of joy. She leaned over and hugged her father. "Thank you," she said. "I won't let you down."

"I know you won't," he said. Then, he closed his eyes and went to sleep.

Russell Walks In

It was the week of Christmas when things took a sudden turn. Nobody had heard from Russell since the night Stephanie last saw him a few weeks earlier.

Stephanie had good intentions to visit Russell after she returned to Maine from college. She cared very deeply about him; however, the unexpected responsibility of running the business was overwhelming. She let herself get caught up in the day-to-day tasks of meeting business needs. There was hardly time for her to sleep.

From his hospital bed, Stephanie's father appointed her as executive manager to handle all of the business decisions and ensure things remained in control. Her mother Melva spent a great deal of time at the hospital with her father. Paul valued her company and needed support through his rehabilitation.

It was the week before Christmas, and it looked like the doctors were going to let Paul go home just in time for the holidays. Tentatively, Christmas Eve looked like it might be the day of his release. However, this would mark the beginning of a long journey through continued rehabilitation. His leg was broken in several places and required additional surgery to help set his bones. It would be many months before he could make a full recovery.

Stephanie was alone at the office on the day before Christmas Eve when she heard the front door open. Jingle bells jingled that hung from the door handle. She stood up from the desk, curious who might have just entered the building. It was late in the day, and nobody was expected. She looked out into the hallway. "Hello?" she called out.

There was no response. She was sure someone had entered the building.

From where she was standing, she could see the light of the sunshine as it passed through the large windows near the front door. There was a silhouette of someone standing there. It seemed creepy. "Hello?" she said, waiting for the person to say something. She was nervous about walking down front to see who was there.

Just then, the man spoke out. "Hi there," he said innocently.

It was Russell. She ran down the hallway to see him.

"How are you doing?" she asked.

He was standing at the front door dressed in nice clothes, and wearing a jacket she had not seen before. He held a Walmart bag in his hands. "I'm fine," he said.

Stephanie felt some guilt for not visiting him since she had returned to Maine.

He said, "I heard through Edna that your father got hurt, and you were running the business now."

Stephanie said, "Yes, it's been quite hectic."

She looked at Russell, surprised by his appearance. He looked good to her.

"Are you here alone?" he asked.

"Yes."

"Good," he said. "I wanted to drop these off." Then, he reached into the Wal-mart bag and pulled out a couple of gifts.

"That's very kind of you," she said. She thought it was odd that Russell had not asked about her father. "Dad's in the hospital," she said.

Russell looked at her. "Yes, I know," he said.

"The doctors say he might be able to come home tomorrow."

"That's wonderful," he replied.

As Russell removed the wrapped gifts from the bag, he looked around for a place he could leave them. There was a small Christmas tree standing next to the door. It had little lights on it but was for decoration only. The floor below it was bare, except for a few pine needles that had fallen off.

Russell asked, "Can I leave these here?'

Stephanie seemed confused why he was acting so distant. She suddenly had the impression that he was avoiding her parents. "Why don't you bring them over to my parents' house?"

He looked down to the floor, as though to avoid making eye contact with her. "I'd rather not be a bother," he said.

"You're no trouble," she replied. "We've all been wondering how you're doing. We can't call you because you don't have a phone."

He looked up at her. "I'm getting one," he said.

"I'm sure my parents would love to see you."

It looked as though Russell was feeling some guilt for not attending his share of the business at Paul's of New England.

"I've had a lot of things to take care of," he said.

She seemed understanding. "Would you like to have a seat?" she asked.

"That's all right. I can't stay long."

When Russell said that, the first thing that came to Stephanie's mind was that he might have found someone to fill the void of not having his father around or family. "Why the hurry?" she asked.

"No particular reason," he said.

She doubted his words. "Then, why leave?" she asked.

Russell sighed. "I don't know."

He sat down in the chair next to the front door and looked around the room. It was quiet. "Boy, it feels weird being here," he said.

Stephanie could see he was missing his father.

"Ever since Dad died, I haven't been able to come around this place."

Stephanie sat quietly, regretting her thoughts about Russell finding someone else to fill the void. She could see he was really a lonely man. His eyes started to water. He tilted his head downward to hide his emotion from Stephanie. She was not sure how to respond.

"I have my good days, and my bad days," he said. Then, after a brief pause, he said, "Today was one of my bad days."

"I wanted to see you sooner," Stephanie said. "I'm sorry I got so busy."

"That's all right; I've been keeping to myself."

Stephanie wanted to tell Russell how much she was missing him after that night a few weeks ago when they shared hot cocoa at his house.

Russell said, "I've missed you."

Stephanie was surprised to hear him say that. Her eyes perked up. "I've missed *you* too," she replied. "I am sorry I didn't go over and see you when I got back."

"That's okay," he said. "Your father needed you. I'm glad you could be there for him." He added, "Besides, I needed some time alone."

Stephanie sat down in the chair next to where Russell was sitting. "I've thought about you a lot," she said.

Russell stood up as if trying to avoid becoming engaged in

a deeply romantic conversation. Avoiding the subject, he said, "When I heard the news of your father, I was hoping everything was going to be okay. I didn't want to interfere."

She did not understand why he said that. "You wouldn't have been interfering with anything," she said. "My father would love to see you." Stephanie went on, "You should go see him."

"I was thinking about it," he said. "Edna saw me in town the other day, and she told me everything."

Suddenly, Russell looked at her with enthusiasm. He seemed excited about something. "Have you heard the news?" he asked.

Stephanie looked confused. "What news?" she asked.

"I've started taking flying lessons," he said.

Stephanie seemed surprised. "What made you do that?" she asked.

"I don't know," he said. "I guess I just needed something for myself."

"Okay."

"Flying is a great outlet for me."

Stephanie agreed. "I think it's good to have a hobby," she said. Then she got the idea of inviting Russell over to her parents' house for Christmas but was not sure how to ask him. "That's great you are doing things for yourself," she said.

Russell nodded in agreement. "Yeah, I needed to do something," he said.

Stephanie looked at him. He seemed chipper to talk about flying. "Would you like to come to my parents' for Christmas?" she asked.

He shut up about flying. "I don't know," he said. "I'm not sure I'm ready for that."

She said, "It would mean a lot to me, and I know my parents would be thrilled to have you join us."

"Really," he asked.

"Yes, and it would mean the world to me."

She had his attention. He was not saying "no," but he was not saying "yes" either.

Then she pleaded with him. "Please, come," she said.

After a brief pause, he said, "All right, I will."

She could not believe it.

That afternoon, she convinced Russell to join her at the hospital to visit with her father and mother. It was something she knew would surprise both of her parents... and it did. When they walked in, Melva was sitting by Paul's side. Both Paul and Melva looked up with eager excitement as they saw who had arrived.

Stephanie jokingly said, "Hey, look who I found."

Melva stood up to greet Russell with open arms and a smile. "Merry Christmas," she said.

Russell cordially said, "Merry Christmas to *you*."

Paul smiled and spoke with a raspy voice. "How are ya' doing?" he asked.

Russell said, "I'm doing all right. Sorry to hear about your mishap."

"Oh, it's one of those things," he said.

Stephanie told her parents that she invited Russell over for Christmas. They thought it was a great idea. He stood quietly as they delighted in the idea of him joining them for Christmas. Russell carried a slight look of guilt on his face, thinking they might be angry with him for not being there to help run the business after Paul's accident. To his surprise, no one said anything about his absence. "We've missed not seeing you," Melva said, and that was that.

Christmas Eve came, and it was late after service at church. Paul, Melva, and Stephanie had returned home in anticipation of Russell's arrival. Paul was very sore and needed assistance to get in and out of the car. He used crutches and had a wheelchair at his house and the church to help him move about. Stephanie sat on the window seat, which was in the front part of their living room. She liked this spot on winter nights because it was near the woodstove, and she could see out the window, as the snow would fall. The weather forecast had called for the evening flurries, but the snow was starting to accumulate. She watched patiently, looking up into the black sky as it spit snow. It was about 9:00 p.m. when the lights of Russell's truck finally came into view.

Stephanie watched as Russell's truck slowly made it up their long driveway. There was excitement in her voice when she turned to her parents and said, "He's here!" She got up from her seat and quickly ran to the front door to greet him.

Russell wore a long coat and a sport cap with leather gloves as Stephanie opened the door. There were a couple of boxes in his arms, and a Wal-mart bag dangling from his wrist. She looked at him and smiled. "Is that the same Wal-mart bag you had the other day?" she asked.

"No, this is a fresh one," he said trying to be funny.

"Won't you come in?"

Melva came to the door. She smiled. "Good evening, Russell," she said.

"Good evening."

Paul looked out from the kitchen with the sound of all the commotion going on. He smiled.

As Russell walked in the front room, he saw Paul sitting there alone in his chair. "Merry Christmas," Russell said.

"Merry Christmas," Paul replied in a soft voice. It was obvious; Paul was still in a lot of pain. Russell could hear it in his voice.

"Thank you for inviting me," Russell said.

Melva reached for Russell's coat to hang it in the nearby closet. "We're glad you could make it," she said.

Stephanie smiled and was excited that Russell had agreed to come over. She knew it would be good for all of them, and it was.

Christmas morning came, and Russell awoke on the couch where he had fallen asleep after enjoying hot cocoa with Stephanie and her parents. Paul slept in the recliner since he was not able to climb stairs.

Stephanie and her mother were out in the kitchen making last minute preparations for dinner. The balsam fir tree decorations sparkled as bight sunshine passed through the ornaments and lit up the room. Beneath, gifts lay wrapped in decorative paper, and there was a fire burning in the woodstove. Paul awoke when Melva came in the room and added wood to the stove. He was sore, but smiled to wake up and know it was Christmas. "Morning," he said. Melva gave him a kiss.

Russell sat up on the couch and said, "Good morning."

Melva and Paul gave Russell a warm welcoming smile. "Good morning," they said.

Stephanie entered the room. "How did you sleep?" she asked Russell.

Russell tried to be funny by putting his head back down on the armrest. "Like this," he said, as he demonstrated *how* he slept.

"Very funny," she said with a smile.

As they were all together in the family room, Paul found the strength to recite the story of Jesus' birth, in keeping with their traditional family Christmas. Stephanie was pleased to see that Russell listened to her father as he quoted scripture from Luke. He talked about the shepherds that came to see the babe wrapped in swaddling clothes lying in a manger: *"And suddenly there was with the angel a multitude of the heavenly host praising*

God, and saying, Glory to God in the highest, and on earth peace, good will toward men" (Luke 2:13–14).

Russell seemed to appreciate hearing the Christmas story, and he appeared grateful to be with Stephanie and her parents. They shared gifts over breakfast, and the day was as all Stephanie had hoped it would be.

New Year's Eve came and went as Russell thought upon New Year resolutions and new beginnings. He spent most of his time alone at the small house and enjoyed studying aviation and learning about airplanes. He remained a student at Maine Instrument Flight in Augusta. Learning to fly airplanes was giving him good exposure to meeting new people, and it helped to take his mind off things.

The business at Paul's of New England continued to run with Stephanie in charge, and she often called home to talk with her father about various building codes and inspections if she was unsure. The supervisors in charge of the construction crews were pleasantly respectful to her and assisted to make her job as easy as possible. Her mother stayed at home on most days so she could attend Paul. Things were going fairly well.

Russell continued to receive quarterly dividends from his father's interest in the company that he had inherited. Paul, Melva, and Stephanie would have appreciated it if Russell had been more willing to help with the business, but they all understood that he had been through a difficult time.

Paul had been home from the hospital since Christmas Eve, and the family was very grateful to have him back. They reflected upon their time spent with Russell, and they prayed for Russell often. At one point, someone from the church initiated a prayer chain for Russell. They all knew he needed guidance and that his coming to the Lord would be in due time. Nobody wanted to pressure Russell into anything. For Stephanie, Russell stood out as a brilliant and shining star. She valued who he was and wanted good things for him.

With Paul's accident, Stephanie realized she would not be returning to college again that year. It frustrated her because she thought God had other plans for her. However, she soon realized God wanted her where she was. She was learning new skills on the job, while her mother was able to help her father in his rehabilitation. Two more surgeries followed the New Year to help Paul get his broken bones in order and heal properly.

Time passed.

With the New Year, Russell knew he needed to make a change in his life. There was a lot of unfinished business in his life. Since his father's death, it meant he was the heir of his father's estate, which was worth a hefty sum. It also meant he now owned one-half of the business. There were concerns about this with the Gallaghers, thinking he might choose to sell his portion of the business. He showed very little interest in working there. It looked as if he just wanted the money. There were reports that he was starting to spend some of his cash. Many of the bills would flow through the office where Stephanie was working. She saw work orders for jobs done at his own personal residences. Russell owned at least three houses; however, he oddly enjoyed spending most of his time at the little house his father had bought. On the few occasions when Stephanie was able to be in contact, he told her he liked the little house mostly because it did not have a telephone. He seemed to be changing… not in a bad way but more centered upon himself. Stephanie would continue to pray for him when she could.

It was a Monday morning in April when Russell walked in to the front office area at Paul's of New England. Julie the receptionist had not seen Russell for months and almost did not recognize him. "Can I help you?" she asked as he walked in.

Russell turned to her and said, "It's me, Russell."

She was surprised to see him. He turned to pour a cup of coffee that was brewing fresh on the coffee maker nearby. Julie noticed Russell appeared to have been taking care of himself as he wore a long dress coat and looked very professional. She wondered if he would be her new boss or if it was still Stephanie. Paul had still not returned to work full-time; however, doctors were saying he was making excellent progress.

Russell walked past Julie's desk with his cup of coffee in hand and then preceded down the hallway. His destination was to find Stephanie, but she was away from her desk. Melva was in her office when Russell walked down the hall. He looked in and saw Melva sitting at her desk. "Good morning," he said.

Melva looked up and seemed surprised to see him. "Well, hey there," she said. "What's happening?"

With a cup of coffee in hand and a smile, Russell said, "I am here to work."

Two workers from the garage down the hall walked by as Russell made his announcement, and they quickly scurried down the hall thinking there was trouble brewing. Everybody knew Russell was a joint heir to the business. Seeing him at work unexpectedly made them nervous of his intentions.

Melva asked, "What is it you'd like to do?"

He stood in her doorway. "I was hoping to find Stephanie," he said.

"I think she's gone to town, but she will be coming right back," she said.

Russell smiled. "Well, I'll wait," he said.

"That would be fine."

Russell turned to look down the hall. He asked Melva, "Is she still working from Paul's office?"

"Yes," Melva said.

"Okay, I'll wait down there." Then, he went into Paul's office and sat down at the desk.

Russell noticed the wall shelf leaning in the corner that was still unfinished. He thought to himself that he might ask one of the employees there to finish it.

Within a short time, he heard the front door open. There were voices talking low, and he was sure Julie was giving Stephanie a warning that he was in the building. Russell heard her voice as she made her way down the hall. She said, "I'm back," as she passed her mother's office.

When Stephanie walked in the room, she was surprised to see Russell. She smiled at him. "What are you doing here?" she asked him.

He sat back in her father's chair. "I'm here to work," he said.

Stephanie paused, seeming to be in disbelief. "Okay… " she said.

Russell smiled at her. She felt he was bluffing.

Then he said to her, "Actually, I'm just kidding. I only came here to tell you that I got my pilot's license."

"Really," she said with intrigue. "That's great." She was happy that he had succeeded in reaching his goal.

"I finally did it," he said.

Stephanie could see he was proud of himself. "I'm glad for you," she said.

He stood up out of the chair. "I was wondering if you might like to go to lunch with me," he asked.

"I'd love to," she replied.

A Dinner Date

More than four months had passed since Paul's accident. He had slowly begun to work back at the office, but only part-time while Stephanie continued to handle most of the administrative tasks. She had become a success in handling business decisions with her maturity.

It was a Friday evening, and Russell invited Stephanie out on a dinner date. They had gone to lunch together numerous times before, but this was to be their first *dinner date.*

Earlier that afternoon, Stephanie had driven her mother's car into town to buy lunch. She was in the car and slowed down to let a few pedestrians pass by. A young couple caught her attention as they passed by the front of the car. They were obviously in love, and seeing them together made her long to have that in her life. She felt her relationship with Russell was good, but she wanted more. He was busy with his own "projects" and with flying. At merely twenty-one years old, she found herself a young career-driven business woman too busy to settle down. She wanted to go back to school in the fall, but she had obligations to the business that needed her as well. She was starting to feel she wanted something more, and she longed to be like the couple she saw walking across the street. It made her sad in a way to think that she may be missing something more that God had planned for her. She was not happy and felt unfulfilled. Working nearly every day of the week was taking its toll on her emotionally. She did not know what she wanted, but she wanted what she knew... and that was love. She had prayed for this so much and had hoped Russell would come to know the Lord. It made it difficult for her to want so much from a man who knew so little about her Lord and Savior. She felt she needed to tell him.

That night, Stephanie and Russell went to an Italian restaurant and ordered up a fabulous meal. It seemed like a perfect evening as the days had begun to get longer with the changing of the seasons. Warmer temperatures were a blessing upon the area, and the snow that had covered the community was melting inch-by-inch every day.

Stephanie sat with Russell in the restaurant and admired his good looks. She thought to herself how easy it would be for any woman to fall in love with him. She *knew* she loved him, and she believed with her heart that she could be happy to spend her life with him. She wondered what it would be like to be his wife. Then, the thought occurred to her that she might not see much of him since he loved flying so much. It seemed like airplanes were all he ever liked to talk about lately. He adored aviation.

The man she once prayed for that she could spend time with had become a reality. She wondered if it was all part of God's plan. There was a romance between them that seemed joyful to her. She wanted to put all things aside for just one evening and talk about salvation. Half way through the meal, she mentioned how important it is to her to have Jesus in her life.

Russell said, "That's fine."

She asked him if he knew Jesus.

Russell said, "I'm all set with that."

The conversation was going as she thought it would. Russell was willing to listen to her talk about the Lord, yet did not fancy himself with believing in God or anything to do with the church.

"I love you," she said to him.

Russell felt good about where their relationship seemed to be heading. He looked at Stephanie from across the small table. "I love you too," he said.

Stephanie said, "That's why it's important for you to know the Bible says you will go to Hell if you do not confess your sins and believe in the Lord Jesus."

Russell seemed bothered by Stephanie's comment. "What do you mean confess my sins? I am living a good life," he said.

She tried to explain what it all meant, but their conversation took a turn for the worse. The meal ended, and he genially took her home. There were no words of anger, just a lack of interest from Russell. Stephanie had trouble understanding why he seemed unmoved to hear the Word of God. As he dropped her off, he almost seemed rude about it.

"Do you want to come in?" she asked.

"No, I've got some things to do at the house."

She was irritated with the way he was acting. "Have fun with your flying," she said sarcastically.

"I will," he replied.

She went in the house and prayed for him.

Feelings Rekindle

It was the first week in May when Stephanie needed to drive out to the Barnes Estate construction site. It was getting late in the day, and this would be her last stop before going home for the night. Her phone rang as she was getting ready to leave the office. To her surprise, it was Russell.

"Hey," he said.

"Hi."

"I'm sorry for last week," he said. "Can I see you sometime?"

Stephanie was in a hurry. "I'm kind of busy," she said.

Russell asked, "Well, when can I see you?"

She replied, "I don't know... some of us have to work for a living."

"That was a cheap shot," he said. "But I deserve it."

She could hear in his voice that he seemed sincerely.

"I have to get some papers signed at a jobsite, and then I'll be going home," she said. "I don't know how late I'll be."

Then Russell surprised her by asking if he could go. "Would you mind?" he asked.

"That would be fine," she said.

They discussed directions, and it was set.

The construction site was located about fifteen miles away and was a place Russell knew well. It was getting dark out by the time she arrived, and she saw Russell standing outside talking to Doctor Barnes, the land developer.

Russell saw her pull into the yard where the large building was under construction. She got out of the car with paperwork in hand. Russell said, "I'll stay out of your way."

Doctor Barnes responded, "It's no trouble."

Stephanie walked up to the parking lot where Doctor Barnes was standing. Russell sat in his truck to wait for Stephanie.

"Good evening, sir," she said to Doctor Barnes.

"Hi, Stephanie," he replied. "Got some paperwork for me?"

"Yes, I do."

"Good," he said. "I've got a check for you."

It seemed that the construction of his new building was going very well. Doctor Barnes was paying for the work in small installments throughout the project, and he enjoyed being a part of the development process, which included visiting the site on a regular basis.

Within minutes, Stephanie and Doctor Barnes completed their transaction. He used the hood of his car to sign the documents. "Thank you," she said as he handed her the paperwork.

"No… thank *you,*" he replied. Then, he got into his car and rolled the window down. "Well, you have a good night," he said.

"You too," Stephanie replied.

Russell got out of his truck to give one last wave "goodbye" to Doctor Barnes.

Doctor Barnes smiled at Stephanie and Russell as he drove off.

Stephanie looked at Russell, curious what he had been talking about with her client. She walked toward Russell. He smiled at her and then proudly said, "He's a pilot."

"Oh," she said as she gathered the paperwork that was in her hands. She seemed pressed for time.

Russell went on about flying. "I met him previously at the airport, actually."

"How nice," she said.

Russell did not seem to notice the undertone of sarcasm in her voice. It was getting quite dark out, and there were very few streetlights around.

"What is it you wanted?" she asked.

Russell said, "I want to apologize for the way I acted last week at dinner."

Stephanie was hoping he had become a believer in the Lord.

"That wasn't me," he said.

Stephanie stood still, looking at him spill his feelings.

"I mean, that was me," he said, "but it wasn't me."

"Okay," she said.

There was a pause. She did not think their conversation would be very productive. She still had a great attraction for Russell but feared he was not ready for commitment. Stephanie gazed up into the star lit sky. It was beautiful that night. "Look up there," she said. "That's God's handiwork."

Russell looked up. "It is beautiful," he said.

"It's peaceful out here," she said.

"Yeah, it is," he replied. "I want to thank you for meeting with me."

"Don't mention it," she said.

A cool chill filled the air.

"I need to go put these things in the car."

Russell suggested, "Why don't you let me take them back to the office for you?"

"No, that's all right."

"No, really," he said, "I insist."

Stephanie thought to herself that he was trying to be on her *good side.* "Okay," she said. "I'll trust you with the paperwork." She knew this would be an open invitation to see Russell again. Although she showed little emotion about being next to him, she was happy inside. She wanted to see if Russell had changed at all.

Russell said, "Let's go ahead and put that stuff in my truck."

"Okay," she said. Then, she turned to walk toward his truck. Russell's attention was on her. She was unaware of it. He watched her open the door and seemed bewildered by her charisma.

"It's a nice view out tonight," he said.

She thought it was strange that he was not helping her put the things in his truck. Where were his manners? She wondered.

"It's a nice view out tonight," he said again.

She turned around to see what he was looking at. He stood there smiling.

"What?" she asked him.

"I said, it's a nice view out tonight. Don't you think?"

"Yeah, I guess," she said, and then turned back around to put the papers in his truck.

Before she could reach inside his truck, Russell was up to his tricks again. She started to get suspicious of his flirting and decided to play along.

"What a nice view tonight," he said.

Stephanie turned back to look at him as if he was starting to lose his mind. "Okay…" she said and then turned to put the papers in the truck.

"See!" Russell said.

Stephanie turned around, and looked back up into the sky. Then she looked at Russell. "Okay, now you're starting to freak me out," she said.

Russell smiled. "Don't let me stop you with that," he said.

She knew what he was doing.

"Can I help you with that?" he asked.

She said, "I'm all set," as she reached inside the truck.

Then Russell walked up to where she was standing. She heard his presence as he neared the truck.

"Let me help you," he said.

Stephanie was enjoying the attention she was receiving from him. She played along with his silly game.

As she turned one last time to reach inside the truck, Russell was standing directly behind her. He tried, seemingly to make himself useful by holding the door open for her. Then he said it again, "Very nice view out tonight."

By now, his comments were starting to get old. She knew what he was doing. She turned her head quickly, hoping to catch a glimpse of him staring at her in a lustful way. As she turned her head, he stood innocently looking up into the star lit night.

"What are you doing?" she asked.

"Oh, nothing," he said.

Stephanie smiled and then stood close to him with her finger pointing to his face. "Well, whatever it is, you better behave yourself," she said.

"I am," he replied.

Just then, Russell looked up into the night sky and inconspicuously began to whistle some kind of lame tune. He obviously had no musical ability. Stephanie liked his playful behavior. She knew it was flirting, but somehow it felt okay. She finally set the papers on the passenger side of his truck.

All of a sudden, she felt a whack across her backside. She turned around quickly and looked at him intensely. "What was that for?" she asked.

"You had a spider crawling on you," Russell said.

"A spider?" she asked. "I don't think spiders are out yet this season."

Russell played along. "It was a spring spider," he said. "It sprung from the ground and jumped on you."

"Okay," she replied.

Thinking two could play at his game, Stephanie said, "What's that big thing crawling in your hair?"

"My hair?" he asked. Then he frantically began shaking his head and scratching his hair to ward out any would-be critters. After a few moments, he stopped shaking his head and then leaned forward to her, holding his head down. "Did I get all the bugs out?" he asked.

Stephanie looked over the top of his head. "It's kind of hard to see in this light," she said. "Come closer."

By this time, Russell almost had his hair in her mouth. "Is it all better?" he asked.

"Looks pretty good to me," she said.

"Thank you," he replied.

She wittingly continued to look into his eyes, and it brought back a familiar feeling of the night they sat alone together on his couch at the small house. She longed to be that close to him again. This was her chance. However, she was nervous about making any advances to Russell that might be unfavorable to God. She knew she felt strongly for him.

"Are you cold?" he asked.

She was about to say "no" but then quickly realized Russell was probably up to one of his games again using this as a tactic to put his arms around her. She wanted to feel his touch, but tried reverse psychology to tantalize him first. "I am freezing," she said.

"Well, I can help you with that," he said.

Stephanie smiled and then handed him the keys to the truck. "You can start the truck so we can get in and get warmed up."

Russell smiled. "Okay," he said.

Amusingly, neither Russell nor Stephanie budged to get into the truck.

"You go first," Russell said.

"No, you," Stephanie replied.

They smiled at each other. Both could feel a difference in their laughter, and the thought of standing there alone on a cold winter night seemed romantic. Stephanie looked at the shirt Russell was wearing covered with lint. "Don't you ever take the fuzzies off your clothes?" she asked.

"No," he said. "Am I supposed to?"

"Yeah," she said.

Russell looked upon his chest to find the lint. "I don't see anything," he said.

She stepped closer to him. "It's right there," she said.

As she reached up to pick the few pieces of lint from Russell's shirt, he stopped her by clasping her hand in his. He held her hand gently and then pulled it close to his heart. He said, "I'm not going to let you steal my lint. They help keep me warm in cold weather."

Stephanie smiled, feeling his gentleness by the warmth of his hand holding hers. Cleverly, she said, "Then if you're not going to let me steal your lint, would you let me steal your heart?"

"Hmmm..." Russell said with a smile, "I'll have to think about that." Then, he looked up into the sky and continued to hold her hand. "There is a nice view tonight," he said.

Stephanie looked up into the sky and giggled. "You said that."

Russell looked down into Stephanie's eyes. "You know, you are the nice view I was referring to," he said.

She smiled as she could feel the warmth of his body next

to hers. It meant a lot to her that he was still holding her hand. "Your hands are so warm," she said.

Russell took a deep breath and felt good about the evening, as his inhibitions to fall in love seemed to subside. "Yes," he said.

Stephanie looked at him. "What?" she asked.

"Yes," Russell said.

Stephanie looked puzzled, wondering if he had just answered the question she asked a few moments ago. She felt as if she had misunderstood what he said. "Yes, what?" she asked.

"Yes, you can steal my heart," he said.

She smiled. "I'll take it," she replied.

At that moment, Russell reached down for her other hand, and he held it close to his heart. She stood silently to see what he was going to do as he held both of her hands with a firm grip. He lifted them up close to his face and then gently kissed the top of her knuckles. "I never had anybody do that before," she said.

"Nobody's ever done that to me either," he said to be funny. As she could not resist, she leaned against his chest, and he wrapped his arms around her.

"I've wanted this for so long," she said.

"Me too," he replied.

That moment felt like a perfect night for Stephanie and one created special for her. In her heart, she knew there would be struggles in her relationship with Russell. It was an unequally yoked union, and one that needed much work. However, for now, she was happy and looked forward to a possible future with Russell.

Stephanie Calls It "Quits"

As Paul returned to work full-time, Stephanie found that she had more free time to herself. She was spending more and more time with Russell. It was May, and the snow that had accumulated upon the land was rapidly melting away as the sun shined brightly with a promising new spring.

One Saturday, she had an argument with Russell because she had asked him to attend church with her and he refused. She had a difficult time understanding how someone who seemingly wanted to be with her showed no interest in the *one* thing that meant so much to her. Talking about her commitment to the Lord was something that never seemed to interest him. She was starting to wonder if he would ever understand how much the church meant to her. It was clear in her mind that he would need to change his ways, or it would be best if they simply remained just friends. She asked him one day, "How can we have a relationship if you never want to come to church?"

"I'm all set with that," he said.

It made her angry that he showed no interest in hearing the Word of God. She had spent so many prayers on Russell, and it was starting to discourage her from trying any further to teach him about salvation. She wondered if he would ever know the way of the Lord. It was something she knew she needed to pray about more. She was getting older and was sure God's plans for her were to return to college in the fall.

The day finally came when Stephanie decided to end her relationship with Russell. It was the month of June and certain to be another summer wasted on a relationship that showed little promise for a bright future. Russell was a "good" man, in her opinion. However, he lacked the one thing that meant so much to her—to know the Lord. Stephanie could accept the fact that her romantic interest might not attend church on a regular basis or even be a member of a congregation; nonetheless, it bothered her that Russell was not even interested in hearing the word. Dragging out such a relationship any further, in her mind, was going against God's will. In addition to this, it bothered her that Russell had become so involved with aviation. It seemed he was spending nearly all of his days at the airport and out flying.

Russell was over at the Gallaghers' house visiting Stephanie when he suddenly needed to leave early. He said to her, "The winds are perfect right now." Then, he reached for their phone to call the airport's automated surface observation system, which reported the latest weather conditions. He said, "The station's reporting calm surface conditions. I need to go."

Stephanie began to get angry. There was sarcasm in her voice. "I think you need to just go pursue your flying since you love it so much," she said.

"What are you saying?" he asked.

"I'm saying, you need to do what you need to do, and I need to do what I need to do."

Russell got the hint where this was going. "What do you mean?" he asked.

"I mean, we can't go on pretending to have a perfect relationship when it's unequally yoked."

"Unequally yoked?" he asked. "I know plenty of couples who are unequally yoked."

"I'm sure," she said. "I know people too, but that's not for me."

Russell looked at her. "So, what you're saying is that you don't want to see me anymore?"

"No," she said. "I love you, and I care about you more than you know. I'm just afraid there will be problems if you can't even bring yourself to church and hear the Word."

Stephanie thought for sure that Russell would be receptive to what she was saying.

"Okay, then," he said. "Be as it may."

Then he left.

Stephanie's eyes began to tear. She sat in the chair in her parents' living room, and she heard his truck start up and drive off. She stood up from the chair and then walked out on the porch. She could see Russell's truck in the distance as he drove through Belgrade Village to the Augusta airport.

Just then, the screen door to the house opened. It was her mother. "Is everything all right?" she asked.

Stephanie replied, "No, everything is *not* all right."

Melva asked, "Is it anything I can help with?"

"No." There was a pause in the conversation as Stephanie stared out across the open lake. She was afraid to turn around where her mother could see that she was crying. She kept her tears to herself and tried to speak as if she was not upset. "I guess I should have been an airplane," she said.

Her mother replied, "Well, don't stay out here too late. We'll be having supper soon."

"Okay."

Stephanie sat on the old wooden rocking chair on the porch

and then lifted her feet up into the chair. She crouched down into the seat with her knees curled up under the overly large sweatshirt she had been wearing that belonged to Russell. He had made her so mad, she wanted to take the sweatshirt off and throw it at him. Of course, she knew she would never do that…but it was an entertaining thought. She held her face down into her shirt for warmth as the evening dew began to set in. Spring was early, and the cool northern air that swept down from Canada sent chills throughout her body. She cuddled in the cold wooden rocking chair and pulled her arms into her shirt for warmth, and she cried to herself quietly, wondering what God's ultimate plan for her would be. She thought she knew, but sometimes she wondered.

In as much as it seemed like a fruitless effort, she sat on the porch chair that evening and prayed for Russell to find salvation. She prayed that he would find somebody who could one day help him understand why it was so important to know the Lord. In her heart, she felt she wanted to give up on him. It seemed obvious that he had to find his own way. She just was not sure how much more discouragement she could take. For her, keeping her acquaintance with Russell as only a *friendship* was the best thing. This would ensure her heart would not be broken again. Still, despite her disappointments, she vowed to herself that she would continue to pray for her friend.

Edna Visits Russell

Russell was going through a hard time in his life. He loved Stephanie passionately and felt a grave imbalance in his life. More than a week had passed since she told him that they could no longer see each other as a couple. The reality of her breakup was more upsetting to him than he thought it would be. He had come to rely on her more than he realized. She not only gave him company, but she also helped him feel secure about himself. Suddenly, the loneliness of not having her around reminded him of when his father died. He felt alone, worthless, and lacked motivation. He had so much to be happy about, but those things were all in material. He had even gone as far as purchasing his own airplane to pass his time. He started to wonder what his life would amount to when it was over. He thought of his father and the large inheritance he had received. Then, it dawned on him that he would have nobody to leave anything for when *he* died. It occurred to him that everything he had amassed would mean nothing. He slept on it and pondered that thought in his heart.

Russell woke up one day angry with himself. He was not only mad because he knew that he had forfeited his relationship with a wonderful woman but also because he felt that the things he owned somehow seemed to own *him.* He wondered if there was any truth in the Word of God.

Russell missed his father, and he wished more than anything that he could have one more chance to see him. He also missed his mother. It had been twenty years since he had seen his mother. He stayed quietly in his small house and cried on the couch where his father once sat and where he enjoyed a cheerful time with Stephanie. He began to feel the dreaded lack of motivation he had before his father's death. Soon, minutes turned into hours, and the hours turned into days. Russell stopped flying his plane as often as he had been. There were times when he even contemplated selling it because it was consuming so much of his time.

A month later, there was a knock at Russell's door. It surprised him because he did not hear anyone drive in the yard. He stood up from the couch after a long night of feeling sorry for himself. He looked out the small kitchen window and saw a silver Honda parked in the driveway. It had rained that night , and the ground appeared damp. It was around noontime, and the sun shined brightly between patchy clouds. He did not recognize the car, but looked to see whose it was. Then, there was the knock at his door again. He could see the silhouette of a woman through the curtains that draped across the door window. He contemplated not answering the door, hoping that the person would go away. The knock grew louder. Then he heard the person speak. "Hello?" she called.

It was Edna.

Russell opened the door for her. "Hi," he said as he stood wearing a T-shirt, shorts, and looking shabby.

"Hello, Russell. How are you?" she asked.

"Good," he replied while rubbing his eyes.

She could see he just woke up. "May I come in?" she asked.

"Sure." Then, he opened the door widely, and she came in.

Thoughts ran through Russell's mind knowing this used to be her house. Somehow, having Edna show up at his door made him feel like some tenant who was under a microscope from the property owner. Russell noticed she was looking around when she entered the room. He looked around and felt embarrassed that he had not cleaned up for a while.

It was obvious to Edna that Russell had been in a depressed state of mind.

"What can I do for you?" he asked as he closed the door behind her.

Edna smiled. "I was hoping there was something I could do for you," she said.

Russell made an effort to show some hospitality. He knew his father always showed good character whenever someone visited. "Please, have a seat," he said, as he pulled out a chair from the kitchen table.

"Thank you," Edna replied. She sat down.

"Can I get you a coffee? Would you like anything to eat?"

"No, thank you," she said. "I don't have a lot of time. I just wanted to come by and see how you were doing."

"I'm doing fine," he said.

"Are you?" she asked.

Russell sat in the chair on the other side of the small table. "As good as I can be, I guess," he said.

"I was hoping I could help you out," she said.

"With what?" he asked.

She said, "People are concerned about you."

"Well, tell them I am fine," he said.

Edna sat quietly for a moment and looked at Russell. It was as if she could see right through him.

Russell said, "I'm just going through a rough time right now."

"I know," Edna replied. "I know what you are going through. I lost my husband fifteen years ago, then my daughter about four years ago, and your father last year."

Russell sat quietly. His eyes started to water.

Russell looked at Edna questioningly... waiting for her next words. "I lost more than just a good friend," she said. "When your father died, a part of me died."

"I don't understand," Russell said.

Edna took a deep breath and sighed. "You see, a lot of people don't know this, but your father and I had plans to spend our lives together."

"Really," he asked. "He never said anything to me about that."

She continued. "He was afraid to tell you because he didn't want you to be upset with him. Your mother meant so much to him, and he tried to set an example for you that *true love* can never die."

Russell sat quietly, taking in all that Edna had to say.

"I can tell you that your father loved you very much, and he never stopped loving your mother. He talked about her all the time. She was a great woman, and I almost feel like I know her."

Russell said, "I don't understand where you're going with this."

"You see," she said. "When my daughter died, a part of me died. When my husband died, a part of me died as well. I am no stranger to heartache and pain. I know the emptiness of loneliness and what it is like to feel alone."

Russell said, "I don't want to be alone."

"You don't need to be," Edna replied.

Russell confided in Edna. She saw him open up to her as a young boy in need of parental guidance. He held his head up, covered by his hands while looking down at the placemat nested beneath his elbows on the table. He began to weep. "I've been such a jerk," he said.

"It's all right," Edna said. "We all have our trials."

Russell cried louder. "No, you don't understand... I've been so bad to everybody that has shown me love."

"You are forgiven," she said. "Go ahead, let it out."

Russell sat at his table and cried. "I just get so confused," he said.

"You are not a bad person," Edna replied. "You are an awesome guy. You are just someone who's been through a lot."

Russell looked up at her as she sat unwearyingly across the table. "I've been through a lot in my life," she said, "and I couldn't honestly sit here and talk with you if I couldn't relate to what you feel inside."

There were tears in her eyes. She looked at him with a motherly instinct. "Trust me," she said. "We all get this way."

Edna felt bad for Russell. "God knows our needs," she said. "He hears our prayers when we come to him. The Bible tells us in the book of John, 'For God so loved the world, that he gave His only begotten son, that whosoever believeth in Him should not parish, but have everlasting life.'"

There was silence in the room.

Russell looked up at Edna. His eyes were wet from crying. "Will you pray for me?" he asked.

"There is nothing in the world I want more to do for you right now," she said.

Then, right there, from Russell's tiny little table where Edna used to sit with her husband, she reached out to hold Russell's hands, and she prayed for him. With eyes closed, she held his hands in hers and prayed aloud. "Dear Lord," she said. "Our hearts are in need. Be with Russell as he seeks to mend his broken ways. He needs guidance, Lord. Help him to know your forgiveness, and live for you. In Jesus' name, I pray."

Russell opened his eyes and looked at Edna. She held on to

his hand. "God is eternal," she said. "He knows us better than we know ourselves."

"I want to do what is right," Russell said.

"It's important that we know our creator, and the eternal life he has promised all of us. All we need to do is believe, and confess our sins to Him."

Russell looked at her with the deepest sincerity. "How will I know when God is working in my life?"

Edna said, "Because you will feel a change in your heart, and you will want to do things that are pleasing to Him."

Russell let go of Edna's hand. She felt there was a change in his heart at that moment.

Russell said to her, "I'm going to try my best."

With that, she told him, "May the Lord bless you." Then, she left.

It was later that evening after the sun set when Russell started to think more of what Edna told him. He watched the sun set over the horizon that night and admired its beauty. The sky was as a large painting put there for him, and he offered thanks to God for it.

As he walked back in his house that night, he sat down and knew in his heart that there had been a change in his life. He believed that there *is* a God…one eternal God in three persons—Father, Son, and the Holy Spirit—and he got down upon his knees and prayed. "Dear Heavenly father, I have sinned against you. Please, come into my heart, and show me the way. Let your love in the name of Jesus Christ lead me to live for you. Help me, Lord, to be strong and do what is pleasing to you. I am in need of a handyman, Lord, who can mend my broken ways. Will you be my handyman, Lord? Help me to be holy. This, I ask in Jesus' name, amen."

Russell fell asleep that night on the couch and felt that he had begun a journey that would last an eternity.

The next day was a Thursday. At the office, Paul and Melva were preparing coffee when the front door opened. They expected that it might be a customer or one of their supervisors reporting to work. When they looked to see who walked in, they were surprised. It was Russell. Paul looked at him with great enthusiasm.

"Good morning," Russell said.

"Good morning," Paul replied. "What a pleasant surprise!"

Russell said, "I'm here."

Melva stood quietly taking it all in. She could see that there was something different about Russell.

Paul said, "It's good to see you."

Russell said, "It's good to see *you.*"

Paul's injuries had healed nicely, and he was getting around fairly well with the use of a cane.

It quickly became obvious to both Paul and Melva that there had been a change in Russell's life. They did not think seriously that Russell was there on business.

Russell said, "What's on our plate?"

Paul looked at his wife, almost asking her if he was seeing what he thought he was seeing. Melva nodded her head as if to say, "Yes… it is so."

Paul asked Russell, "I beg your pardon?"

"I'm here to work," Russell said. "That is, if you can use on old reformed geezer."

Paul looked into Russell's eyes, and then nodded his head "yes." He smiled and then looked back at Melva. Russell stood eagerly waiting to have something to do. Paul smiled at Russell and held his hand out to shake Russell's hand. "It's good to have you back, old buddy." It was as if Paul could see something in Russell, and it reminded him of Alan. Both Paul and Melva sensed that Russell came to know the Lord as it became prominent in his demeanor.

"What shall I work on today?" Russell asked.

"I am so glad you asked that," Paul said. "We've got a ton of good projects happening."

Russell smiled. "All right then," he said. "Let's get to work."

Melva left the room to call Stephanie and tell her of the good news. She knew this was what they had prayed for all along.

The Plane Ride

The Gallaghers were beginning to have Russell over for dinner on an almost nightly basis. Stephanie was becoming very fond of the changes that Russell had made in his life. Likewise, Russell had begun to attend church regularly. He was excited about his newfound faith in the Lord Jesus Christ. Russell had grown to love the Lord, and he was sure of his salvation because he found it in his heart to put the foolish things of his past away. He had confessed his sins to the Lord and had new reasons to live a better life. Pastor James even baptized Russell in the local stream that ran past a nearby farm. Everyone from the church attended Russell's dedication service, and Stephanie was there in the front pew to take his picture. He received a warm welcome from the congregation, and the church sung hymns in celebration of Russell's faith.

In addition to Russell's new life as a Christian man, he had become a very experienced pilot.

It had been several years since Steve's parents died in a plane crash, and Edna saw the possibility of asking Russell at church if he would give her grandson a ride in his airplane to help Stevie put closure on his parents' deaths. The first time she mentioned the idea to Steve he was unsure if a ride in an airplane would be a good idea, but a sermon from Pastor James one Sunday morning helped Steve have a different perspective on life. It was at the close of service when Steve and his grandmother were exiting the church, and he looked up at his grandmother and said, "I'll do it."

It had been nearly a month since Edna first suggested the idea of flying to him. She had forgotten about their conversation. "Do what?" she asked.

"I would like to go flying," Steve said.

Edna smiled. "We can arrange that."

Later that week, she called upon Russell who had been making a positive impact at Paul's of New England. Of course, he was more than delighted to give the boy a ride. A date was set, and Steve had a flight planned just for him.

On the day of the flight, Edna and Steve were pleasantly surprised as Russell and Stephanie stood outside of the fence at the Augusta State Airport waiting for them to arrive. Russell kept his plane in one of the hangars at Maine Instrument Flight. They watched as Edna and Steve drove into the parking lot and then walked out to greet them.

Russell and Stephanie approached the car. Steve was the first one to get out.

Russell said, "Good morning!"

Edna was next to get out of the car. She had a camera in her hands and smiled to see Stephanie standing next to Russell. "Good morning, you two," she said.

Russell smiled back. "Nice to see you," he said. "We're glad you could make it."

"What a pleasant surprise!" Edna said. It quickly became apparent that she seemed happy to see Stephanie with Russell. "We're here!" she said with some enthusiasm.

"Today is a perfect day to fly," Russell said, as he looked up into a clear blue sky.

They stood in the parking lot as Steve watched an airplane land out across the runway. He seemed nervous to fly but in high spirits. Russell noticed the boy's excitement. "So you want to go flying today?" he asked.

Steve said, "Oh yeah."

It was a busy Saturday at the airport as aircraft of all shapes and sizes taxied by. There were planes parked on the other side of the fence, and Steve's attention drew to figure out which plane he would be flying that day. "Which plane is yours?" he asked Russell.

Russell said, "It's parked around the corner. You can't see it from here, but we'll go in soon."

Edna said, "I'd like to get a picture of you three together before we go in."

It caught Russell by surprise to hear Edna say those words. He was sure she was trying to see if he and Stephanie were close, as a couple. He went along with the photo idea.

Edna held her camera up, and she steadied the lens. Russell, Stephanie, and Steve stood with the backdrop of the Maine Instrument Flight building in the background. "Could I get you all to move in a little closer?' she asked.

Russell stood in a static position as Stephanie and Steve moved in closer. Stephanie stood next to Russell while young Steve stood in the front of them. Edna took the picture and seemed happy with the way it came out.

Russell led the small group to the access gate, where he slid his proxy card into the machine. The gate opened, and Steve's excitement grew with each second. As the gate closed behind them, Russell added, "I've already been up buzzing around this morning. It should be a good flight for us." Then, they walked toward the ramp where his plane was.

Steve seemed amazed by some of the planes parked nearby. It was almost overwhelming to him. This was his first time seeing aircraft so close. As they made their way over to the edge of the hangar, Russell's plane came into sight. Steve's eyes lit up with enthusiasm. Russell's airplane was a lot sleeker than Steve had imagined.

Russell said, "That's a Diamond four-two."

Steve looked at it as he approached the plane. It was white with two engines, one on each wing, and the main wings swooped at the tips with prestigious winglets that pointed upward. The tail number was N777SG.

Steve asked Russell what the numbers on the side of the plane meant. Russell replied, "The 'N' is November," he said, "and the three sevens are because I love the Lord."

"What does SG stand for?" Steve asked.

Edna smiled looking at Russell.

Russell put his hand on Steve's shoulder. "SG are the initials to a very special girl," he said as he looked at Stephanie. "Are you sure you want to go flying today?" he asked.

Steve replied, "More than ever."

"Okay," Russell said. "Let's go."

Edna asked Steve if he wanted her to go with him. He replied, "No."

Stephanie helped Russell lift the canopy that opened up the cockpit to the airplane.

"I'm going to have you sit up front with me," Russell said. "You'll be over here on the right side."

Stephanie gave Russell a kiss on the cheek. "I'll be over there waiting with Edna," she said.

"See you when we get back," Russell said.

Steve was the first to climb in the passenger seat, and Russell helped him buckle in safely.

Edna stood near the airport hangar as Russell started one of the two engines. A few moments later, he started the other engine. This was very exciting for Steve.

Steve watched Russell as he went through all the sophisticated instruments that were crammed in the front panel. It was overwhelming. "Wow," he said.

They sat patiently as Russell conducted a pre-flight check of all the instruments. He talked to Steve throughout the process. "You see, we check everything over before each flight. Things need to be safe, or we don't fly."

Russell called for a radio check. "Augusta Unicom, twin star, seven, Sierra, Golf, radio check, please."

Just then, a voice came over the radio. "You're loud and clear seven, Sierra, Golf."

Steve smiled and talked with Russell through the headset wired into the instrument panel. Steve could hear everything going on with air traffic control, and then they taxied up to the run-up area. Steve waved to his grandmother as they taxied by. Russell looked at Stephanie and smiled as she stood next to the hangar. For the first time, Stephanie looked proud of Russell's accomplishment for becoming a licensed pilot. He had achieved a commercial rating, and certified to fly in instrument conditions where visibility was zero. It was a greater accomplishment than she once realized, and it meant something to her that he had stayed with his hobby.

Russell called out, "Augusta traffic… twin star, seven, seven, seven, Sierra, Golf taxiing for departure three-five, Augusta," and then they slowly entered onto the runway in position.

Prior to take-off, Russell looked over at Steve and said, "How are you feeling, my buddy?"

"Good!" Steve replied.

Russell quickly realized he was acting as a father figure to Steve. He turned his eyes on the runway, and then called out. "Augusta traffic… twin star, seven, Sierra, Golf is rolling three-five, Augusta," and then he powered up the engines to full throttle. The aircraft quickly accelerated down the runway and lifted off within seconds.

Steve was calm and relaxed throughout the entire flight. They flew over the city of Augusta, and passed over the state capitol building before circling back around over the Augusta Civic Center and Wal-mart. Steve recognized the skate park down near the waterfront as the Kennebec River flowed from northern towns all the way down to coastal areas of the Atlantic Ocean. Russell talked with Steve throughout every aspect of the flight. "We're going to climb to a thousand feet, then leave the area to the west," he said, as he pointed left. The plane climbed to altitude smoothly, and there was hardly a wind-pocket felt as Russell navigated over nearby lakes and streams. This was the pinnacle of Steve's trip, to see his home from the air. They also passed over the schools he had attended and the small country church that he knew so well.

On the way back to the airport, Russell surprised Steve with something that he never expected. "How would you like to take the stick?" he asked.

Steve looked up at Russell as he flew the plane effortlessly. "You mean, right now?" he asked.

"Yeah, right now," Russell replied.

Steve seemed a little nervous about it but wanted to try. Russell explained what to do. There were two control sticks from the front part of the leather seats. Both were in synchronization with each other.

Russell said, "You just go ahead and put your right hand on the stick. I am going to hang on over here. Do it gentle now."

Steve excitedly held the stick in his right hand as Russell instructed. Russell coached him about the control inputs and how to add gentle movements. Within minutes, Steve had the hang of maneuvering the airplane in straight and level flight. Russell explained how to make soft gentle turns left and to the right, and Steve had no difficulty with that. He managed to keep the plane in coordinated flight using the rudder pedals and impressed Russell with his first-time ability.

Within about an hour, the two headed back to the Augusta State Airport. They entered the left downwind for runway three-five at a forty-five degree angle and flew the air-traffic pattern to left base and then final approach. It had been the best time of Steve's life.

On the ground, he thanked Russell for the ride. Edna smiled as she looked at Stephanie. It was a good day for all of them. Edna felt in her heart that Steve had made a connection and possibly might be able to put closure on his parents' deaths. Steve knew nothing on earth could ever bring his parents back, but he felt something within himself that seemingly gave him a sense of the love they had for him on the day they perished. For nearly five years, he had felt empty inside without having the chance to put closure on his parents' deaths. He had regretted not being able to see them on the day they died. All at once, he realized that he *was* with them on the day they died. He was with them in their hearts, and he was sure that he would have the chance to see them again in heaven. Steve knew the Lord well.

At the end of the day, Russell reflected back on his time with Steve, and Stephanie was proud of Russell for all the changes he had made in his life. He drove her home that evening and dropped her off at her parents' house. They both knew the end of summer was near, which meant Stephanie would be returning to college. This, she thought, was what God had planned for her.

Epilogue

It was the very night before Stephanie was due to fly back to Madison, Wisconsin, for another year of college when Russell called her and asked her out to dinner. She was curious about his sudden need to see her. They had already said "goodbye" for the season and agreed to remain friends. Russell was busy with projects at Paul's of New England, and his schedule unfortunately was not going to allow him to see her off at the airport when she left... so she thought.

Plans were set for her parents to drive her down to Portland International Jetport on Saturday. However, Russell woke up that Friday morning and knew what he needed to do. It was something he had contemplated before yet never had the courage to do. Marriage was something he thought was for other people. Somehow, his experience of having Jesus in his heart and living for the Lord helped him realize what he wanted out of life. He knew asking Stephanie to marry him would be a far-fetched idea, but he felt in his heart the blessings he had experienced in his life because of her. He was grateful to know who she was and came to the realization that he would never meet anyone else like her. It made him feel empty to know she would be gone for another year at college. He loved her eternally, and although he knew the thought of her accepting his marriage proposal was not likely, he felt he owed it to her to tell the world that he loved her. He woke up that day and rushed into the office just to get things started. Stephanie was home at her parents' house preparing for her big trip. He called her and asked if she would go to dinner with him… just for "old times" sake. She accepted. That was when everything changed.

Russell took the rest of the afternoon off from work. He drove down to the local jewelry shop on Water Street in Augusta where he picked out an engagement ring. The clerk was very helpful to him and congratulated him on his undertaking. He returned to his truck, parallel parked along the street out in front of the store. When he got in the cab and closed the door, he held the ring in his hand and prayed to God. "Lord… I may fall, I may stumble… I may do a lot of things that are not always for the best, but help me be what You want me to be, and to be a support in Stephanie's life. Even if all we remain is friends, I only want her to know how much she means to me and that I love her. In Jesus' name, I pray. Amen."

With that, Russell started his truck and then went home to get ready.

The sun was setting behind the trees that stood tall in the backyard of the Gallaghers' home when Russell drove in. Stephanie was sitting in the window seat reading a book when Russell drove in. He saw her in the window as he pulled up along the front porch. She opened the front door for him and let him in the house.

In the kitchen, Melva was preparing a ham for dinner. "Hello, Russell," she said.

"Good evening," he said politely.

Stephanie looked at him. "I'm all ready to go," she said.

Russell took her hand as they stood in the foyer. "Would you excuse me for a few moments while I go talk with your parents?" he asked.

"Sure," she replied looking dazed and confused.

Melva heard a part of the conversation. She turned the stove down low as though she knew what was to come. As she wiped her hands with a hand towel, she looked in the foyer. "Do you want me to holler to Paul?" she asked.

Russell looked at Stephanie. "This won't take that long… I don't think," he said. Then, he turned to Melva and asked if he could see her and Paul in private.

Stephanie wondered what sort of tricks he might be planning. She was curious but not worried. There were bigger, better things to think about in her mind… she thought.

Melva said, "Let's go in the backyard. I think Paul's in the swing."

Stephanie sat down on the wooden rocking chair that sat on the porch all year long. She sat patiently while Russell and her mother went into the backyard to see her father.

Paul was surprised to see Melva and Russell walking into the backyard as he tried to relax on the family bench swing. Russell was dressed nicely and looked a little nervous about something. Melva had a peculiar, suspicious look about her. It seemed like she was in on the surprise, whatever it was. Paul was curious why Stephanie was not with them. "Is everything all right?" he asked.

Melva smiled. "Everything is fine," she said. It was as if she knew what Russell was doing.

Paul stood up from the bench swing. "Would you two like to sit down?" he asked.

Russell looked at Melva, as if to ask her permission if it was okay to sit on the swing. She smiled at him. Russell looked at

Paul. "Sure," he said. "I'll have a seat." He sat down, and Melva joined him as she gave Paul a quick wink with one eye.

Paul was catching on to what was about to happen. He sat down on the other side of the swing where he had been reading a magazine. He set it down on the bench to hear what Russell had to say. "What seems to be the trouble?" he asked Russell.

Russell spoke nervously. "There's no trouble," he said. "Stephanie's out front on the porch waiting for me."

"Well, let's not keep her waiting too long," Paul replied. "What is it we can do for you?"

"Actually," Russell said, "I am here because I wanted you to know that I went into town today and bought a ring for your daughter, and we're about to go out to dinner and I wouldn't feel right about asking her to marry me unless it met with your approval."

Paul looked down and clasped his hands together in his lap. "I see," he said. Then, he looked at Melva. "Is this something you knew about?" he asked her.

She looked at him. "No, it's news to me." Melva looked pleased by the notion of Russell taking her daughter's hand in marriage.

Paul sat quietly, as if trying to torture Russell with anticipation. He looked up at Russell. "And you expect that she'll accept?" he asked.

Russell said, "Well, actually I don't know if she'll want to marry me. I love her with all my heart. I just can't bear the thought of her going back to school tomorrow without at least knowing how much she means to me."

"I see," Paul said. He seemed to be a world of questions, as any concerned guardian would be. "And asking her to marry you is the answer?"

Russell thought for a moment that he might not be able to

meet Paul's expectations. He was not quite sure how to respond to the question.

"Let me ask you again," Paul said. "Do you think asking Stephanie to marry you is the answer?"

Again, Russell felt dumbfounded by Paul's question. He thought about it for a moment, fearing that Stephanie's father was not going to approve of his daughter marrying him. Then, he thought about what was in his heart. "Well, yes, sir, I do," he said. "There is nothing I want more than to have the opportunity to spend each and every day of my life with her."

Paul looked back down at his hands as he twiddled his thumbs. "I see," he said. Then, he looked over toward Melva, who had remained quiet throughout the conversation.

Russell was sure he was about to leave without having approval from Stephanie's parents to marry her. In his mind, he knew it was a reality of everyday life, and in time... perhaps, he could prove himself worthy to them.

Just then, Paul said to Russell, "I think you better get going."

Russell looked sorrowful but kept his head up. He showed good character by acting maturely to the *presumed* disappointment he was apparently receiving. He looked at Paul and Melva. "I thank you for your time," he said.

Paul looked at Russell, and then held his hand out to shake his hand. "I thank you for *your* time... son," he said.

Russell looked at Paul confused as he stood up from the swing. He held his hand out to Paul wondering if he heard correctly when Paul said "son."

Paul smiled at Russell. "Welcome to the family," he said.

Russell's face lit up with exhilaration. "Do you mean it?" he asked.

Paul said, "There is nothing we want more than to know Stephanie is marrying a man who will be good to her. We have known you for most of your life, and I cannot think of anybody who would be better for her. Of course, it will be up to her if she wants to marry you, but you have our blessing."

Russell was more excited than he could ever remember. "I won't let you folks down," he said.

Melva replied, "We know you won't." Then she proceeded to give him a hug.

Paul also gave Russell a hug. "We'll be praying for you… for both of you," he said.

"Thank you."

Stephanie was patiently waiting out front on the rocking chair when Russell slowly opened the front screen door to the house. He smiled at her as he walked out onto the porch.

"How did it go?" Stephanie asked.

Russell looked happy inside about something, but he did not want to tell her what it was. "It went well," he said.

"That's good," she replied. "Where are you taking me?"

"Olive Garden," he replied.

"That works," she said.

The drive into town was relaxed as Stephanie thought about the day that would follow. College was ahead of her, and her bags were packed. The airline tickets and everything were in order. She thought Russell's behavior was peculiar why he desperately *needed* to take her out to dinner that night. Supposedly, he was going to be "busy." However, there had been some sudden change. She was curious and somehow happy to go along for the ride.

That night, over dinner at the Olive Garden, Russell continued to act capricious. This was not his usual character, and Stephanie jokingly wondered to herself if maybe Russell had hit his head on the airplane's canopy when he got out of the plane.

Russell looked a little nervous about something and preoccupied by others in the restaurant. There was a good crowd there because it was Saturday night. Then, Russell sat still for a moment with his hands over his face. It appeared he had something to say.

"What is it?" Stephanie asked. By now, the suspense was starting to get the best of her.

"All right, I'll tell you," Russell said. Then he stood up in his chair and looked around the room. "Excuse me," he said looking at others sitting in the nearby tables. "Excuse me," he said again. "May I briefly have you attention?" he asked.

The chatter in the restaurant quieted down. Stephanie did not know what to think. She crouched down in her chair thinking this could not be happening. It was somewhere between embarrassing and exciting.

Russell said openly, "I have an announcement to make." Then he looked at Stephanie and knelt down before her.

She was in disbelief.

"Stephanie," he said. "I love you." Then he reached into his coat pocket and pulled out what appeared to be an engagement ring. As he opened the lid to the tiny gray box, he proceeded to say, "I would be so honored if you would have me as your husband. Would you marry me?"

It was a surreal moment and one Stephanie could not believe. She stuttered to find the words, and tears quickly came to her eyes. "There is nothing I want more than to be your wife," she said.

With that, Russell held her hands to his lips and kissed them.

Everyone in the restaurant applauded as the news quickly spread from table to table that the man and woman had just become engaged to be married. Patrons standing in the lobby heard the noise, and they too applauded.

Stephanie chose not to return to college that year. It became apparent to her that God's plan for her was *not* what she had thought it was all those years. She came to realize that God's plan was Russell, and she knew in her heart what she needed to do. College, for the moment, would have to wait indefinitely so she could focus on a life with Russell and grow with him in his faith as they established a new life together and in worked within their church. This, she knew, was what God had planned for her all along.

Stephanie said to Russell one Sunday morning, as they were preparing for church, "I have a confession to make."

He looked at her precariously, curious to what she had to say. He smiled. Then, in his trusting voice asked, "What is it?"

She smiled at him and then paused briefly as though trying to find the words.

Russell had a look of ten thousand questions on his face. "Okay, you've got my attention," he said.

She did not say anything immediately; rather she smiled to tantalize him a little longer in suspense. "Do you remember that day in the hospital when your father whispered something in my ear?" she asked.

Russell thought back. "How can I forget?" he asked. "That was the day Dad died."

"Well," she said, "I never told you this because I was always afraid to bring it up."

Russell looked at her. "You don't need to worry about offending me with anything," he said.

"That day he whispered to me," she said, "he asked me if I would marry you… if you ever asked me, and I told him I would. I never dared tell you because I didn't know if I wanted to marry you or not."

Russell paused, looking surprised with what she was saying. "Wow," he said. "I never knew that."

Stephanie stood looking slightly nervous about the reaction she was expecting from Russell.

He thought about it for a moment, and then said, "I always knew I could be happy with you. I was just never happy with myself," he said. "I needed time to figure things out for myself. You helped show me the way, and I am so grateful for that. If anything ever comes between us, I will always know it was your love and prayers that helped make me who I am today, and I believe I am a better person today because of you. I do not expect every day of our lives to be perfect, but I know with whatever life brings, the Lord is our shepherd. Just as Pastor James read to us Psalm 23 on the day Dad died, I knew then that I needed to make a change in my life."

Stephanie looked at him with a confused looked. "I don't understand," she said. "When your father died, and my dad suggested that we rejoice in the Lord, you left the room. I thought it was because you did not believe in the Lord."

Russell said, "No. I left the room that day because when Pastor James read Psalm 23, it was as though God spoke to me that day. It was then, that I started to believe."

Stephanie could not believe her ears. "I never knew this," she said.

"I'm sorry, I never told you. I left the room that day because I knew right then and there that I would need to make a change in my life. I started reading my father's Bible, and things started to make sense to me but I was not ready to make any commitment."

"Why didn't you just ask me or my parents?" Stephanie asked curiously.

"Because," he said, "the last thing I wanted was for you or your parents to think I wanted to be saved to win you over. I had to find my own way. It was more of a personal thing. I was afraid to make any commitment. I had no idea that's what Dad whispered in your ear that day."

Stephanie said, "I guess we never know what God has planned for us until He's ready for it to happen."

Russell nodded his head. "I would agree," he said.

Stephanie and Russell were married in the spring and purchased a home together on Salmon Pond in Belgrade, Maine, not far from where she had grown up. It was less than a year later when their first child, Michael Alan Holland, was born. With another baby on the way, Stephanie became a stay-at-home-mom while Russell managed the family business. Both remained active in their church. Stephanie continued as a youth group leader, and Russell became active in serving as a leader for the adult Sunday school class. A year later, the church nominating committee elected him as a deacon, and he gladly accepted the responsibilities.

Years later, Stephanie and Russell purchased her parents' share of the business, while Paul and Melva retired. Life trials and tribulations would come and go; however, they found a peace within their hearts that money could not buy. They were happy in knowing that they had each other, their children, their church, and were equally involved in their service to the Lord.

Song Title and Credits:

Carl Boberg, "How Great Thou Art"

W.H. Clark, Ralph E. Hudson, "Blessed Be the Name"

Frederick W. Faber, Henri F. Hemy, "Faith of Our Fathers"

About the Authors

Thomas-john Veilleux, who grew up in Maine, Louisiana, and Missouri, always had a passion for aviation and writing. Today, he is a free-lance writer, former deacon, and member of his local church. He currently resides in Mount Vernon, Maine, with his wife and their two small children where he enjoys spending time with family, friends, and flying. He enjoys writing stories drawn from real-life experiences and is always looking for the next adventure!

Beth Bulmer-Sirois continues to write stories drawn from real-life experiences. She attends church at the same place she has been to since she was an infant. With past experience as a Sunday school teacher and youth group leader, some of Beth's favorite activities include organizing Easter morning services, studying God's Word, and working with the teen groups. Many of her projects give her the opportunity to write, and she continues to develop her skills as a writer. She continues to be actively involved with the church and enjoys spending time with her children, grandchildren, and many friends. She resides in Mount Vernon, Maine.